Green f

or Danger

Byker Grove
GREEN FOR DANGER
Don Webb

BBC BOOKS

To Jemma Trevor, with love.

BYKER GROVE is a
Zenith North Production

Published by BBC Books,
a division of BBC Enterprises Limited,
Woodlands, 80 Wood Lane, London W12 0TT
First published 1991
© Don Webb 1991
ISBN 0 563 36260 X
Set in Baskerville by Redwood Press Limited, Melksham, Wiltshire
Printed and bound in Great Britain by Clays Ltd, St Ives plc
Cover printed by Clays Ltd, St Ives plc

CONTENTS

CHAPTER ONE

Winston is small and has never thought of himself as any kind of athlete. He tends to duck out of P.E. or anything that requires running or jumping. He's like a lot of us. He would like to be able to run faster, but he's never done anything about it. Which leaves him with the rest of his life to think about what might have happened if he had just been able to run a little bit faster the night he pinched the newspaper off the delivery boy's bike and read with mounting relief that he and Gill hadn't killed anybody the night they had stolen the big car to go on a skidding joy-ride. The joy in his heart was pumping through his body as he ran as fast as he could to tell Gill the good news.

To be fair to Winston, he was probably running faster than he'd ever run before and even if he'd been able to go twice as fast, he probably wouldn't have been able to stop Gill, or even make him hear what he had to say. He got to the garage just as Gill gunned the engine hard and spitefully swept the big, hideous foreign car out of the gate and straight on to the main road. Winston could only watch and wave the useless newspaper and then watch again as Gill took his eyes off the road for just a tiny moment. A moment which was long enough to send the car crunching under a lorry, smashing the roof down on top of his best and only friend and squeezing the whole car down much too far for any human being to have any chance at all.

The rest of what happened that night was just fright and tears and the blue lights of the police cars and the ambulances. And, much later on, in the stupid shiny hospital with a cup of coffee clutched in his hand, it was Geoff's arm round his shoulders and Geoff's tear dripping on his head that told him he should have run much, much faster. He had never stopped blaming himself. He probably never would.

Half the time, he blamed Julie too. If she hadn't gone away, Gill wouldn't have gone looking for her. Deep down inside he knew that wasn't fair. But Gill was dead and that wasn't fair either.

They had the funeral and all the girls cried buckets, even the ones who hadn't liked Gill much. In fact they were the ones who cried most of all. And Donna Bell wore a black ribbon in her hair for a bit until she decided it made her complexion look like tripe. Those that grieved most, grieved inside, Winston most of all. Julie, and nobody could believe this, didn't even come to the funeral. It wasn't like her, that much they knew, and Donna felt certain that she had gone into a decline and taken to a sick bed.

'She'll probably end up like that mad old biddy in a wedding dress surrounded by cobwebs in that picture,' she confided to Nicola, whose only answer was to roll her eyes, this being the best way to deal with Donna's more lurid flights of fancy.

Nobody had been able to find Gill's father. Geoff made some enquiries and Bob Grant, the community policeman, put out some feelers and there was a sort of message that he had gone to Ireland but the trail petered out and it was Byker Grove that saw to the funeral. Actually it was Geoff and Alison and Brad and the parents who dug in their pockets. Geoff also went to see the man who owned the garage and who had sacked Gill. But he was more concerned about the car and Geoff only just managed to come away without throttling him.

There was no money for a tombstone, or a memorial, although there was a certain amount of talk, as there always is when things like this happen. Nothing got done and Geoff was just as happy to let it slide, being more interested in the living. Let the dead past bury its dead. Children have to learn to deal with grief and mourning but it should brush them lightly. They shouldn't be weighed down with it.

Winston had other ideas. He collected some big white stone pebbles and picked out Gill's name and the date on the little mound over his grave. And, as often as he could, he took some flowers. The first time he went, he took a little vase but that got smashed so, after that, he just left the flowers.

He knew Gill was dead but he wasn't quite sure what that meant. He didn't go to church, so he had nobody to ask. He just thought about the fact that one day Gill had been there, alive and warm and moving with that special, dare-devil glint in his eye. And now ... there was nothing left.

Winston knew Gill had left his body but he didn't understand how the soul fitted in. He knew there was a special part inside everybody, the thinking part that was more than a brain; the part that could look into a mirror and say quietly to itself, 'Who am I?' And then search the eyes in the mirror and wonder. But Winston had never been able to do that for long without a very weird feeling creeping over him. At which point, he would brush his teeth very hard and wash his hands noisily and rush down the stairs to be as near normal as he could get these days.

He had tried to open up the subject with Kelly once. She had listened carefully to what he was trying to say and then said quite simply, 'Gill's dead and the sooner you fix that in your mind and get on with living your life, the better for you and me and everybody concerned!'

Winston had nodded philosophically and gone about his business and hadn't sought to involve Kelly again. But he caught her worried looks from time to time when she thought he hadn't noticed her watching him.

Months went by and it was a sort of standstill time. Two lots of holidays came and went. People were around and it was a good summer with little outings and rituals and fallings out and makings up. The end of the summer started to arrive, and leaves blew about.

Winston kept up his solitary outings to the graveyard and

on more than one occasion he was noticed by a minister, there on professional matters with funerals and brooding relatives. He saw the waif-like figure on the skyline a couple of times and each time he resolved to talk to him and find out what drew the boy to a grave two or three times a week. But somehow he never did, until the day he came quite suddenly round the corner and bumped into Winston kneeling by the grave. He was just about to speak when he realised that Winston was looking behind him and he turned to see a startlingly attractive young girl, whose eyes were fixed on the shabby little grave. He stopped and then walked past quickly, uncomfortable in the presence of such sorrow.

He turned just once, at the edge of a line of wind-whipped bushes. The girl's head was down and, although Mr Skerrett, the man of God, could not hear the boy's words, his gestures and expression were bitter.

'I'm sorry,' said Julie Warner. Her voice broke a little as she saw the sadness etched on Winston's face. 'I'm sorry,' she said again.

'Aye,' he nodded, and started to turn away.

She looked again at the little grave, all that was left of the boy who had loved her and had stolen a car to come and see her and had been killed before the journey had even started. Her heart filled up when she saw his name picked out in small stones and she wanted to put her arms round Winston but a look at his small, hard, unforgiving face stopped her.

'Did you do this?' she said. 'Put Gill's name?' And he nodded yes.

'We couldn't afford a gravestone,' he added. 'The funeral took all the money. I just put these pebbles so people would know who it was here.' He looked at her again and she was uncomfortable and defensive.

'I'm sorry,' she said again, knowing as she said it that it wasn't enough for Winston, and would never be enough for

10

her either. Winston carried on looking at her for a second and then turned away.

'What could I have done?' she screamed at him and the noise of her voice startled the rooks in the nearby trees so that they launched themselves unsteadily into the wind, lurching and calling to each other, black against the sky. Winston turned and looked at her. When he spoke, his words were deadly and truthful and hurt her so much that all she could do at first was wince.

'All he had was you,' said Winston. 'He never had anything in his whole life except you. No mam, no dad, no brothers, sisters. Just you. You could have stopped him.' She shook her head. He looked at her again and spoke again just as truthfully, just as hurtfully. 'If you hadn't of went away,' said Winston slowly, 'Gill would never have had the crash. Gill would be alive now.'

Julie shook her head again. 'That's cruel, Winston,' she said. 'That's cruel.'

'Aye,' said Winston. 'Aye, it is. And it's true.' And he walked away, his head down and the hot, salt tears fighting their way out through his eyelids and sliding cold down his cheeks. And Julie stood and watched him go and suddenly broke down herself. She kneeled down in the sparse grass by the side of the little scruffy mound and patted the earth.

'Oh, Gill,' she whispered. 'Oh, Gill. I'm sorry. But I couldn't have stayed. I couldn't. Not even for you.'

At Byker Grove, Spuggie was having the mother of all rows with her big brother. Fraser had astounded everybody but himself by doing very well in the summer exams. Because of this, Spuggie had assumed (and had already boasted to Joanne, her newest best friend) that Fraser would be going to university and probably end up as a lawyer or something. And then Fraser, behaving as stupidly as only big brothers

11

can, had dropped his bombshell. Spuggie couldn't believe what she was hearing.

'What?' she shouted. 'What?'

'I'm leaving school and I'm getting a job,' Fraser asserted blandly.

'Why?' she shouted again, and his bland, Fraser-like reply made her want to kick his shins. He was so sensible and stupid and predictable. And you couldn't argue with him, ever.

'We have no money coming in,' he said. 'Do you want to be fostered for the rest of your life?'

And with that one question he had her. It was Spuggie's greatest fear that her mother would never come out of the alcoholics' rehab unit. And, though Lou and Nick who ran the foster home were the nicest people she had ever met, sometimes she still cried softly in the night for her mam.

Just then she spotted Geoff chuntering out of the Grove. Actually Geoff often chuntered out of the Grove at very appropriate times. Spuggie grabbed his arm. He looked and – as always when he saw Spuggie – he grinned.

'What's going on here?' said Geoff.

Spuggie pointed angrily at Fraser. 'Will you talk to this great fat stupid wally?' she said, and Fraser grinned at Geoff over the top of her head.

'What about?' said Geoff, grinning back.

So she told him and Geoff stopped grinning. He knew all about the pressure to get a job, any job, and how bright kids like Fraser were often cheated by the system out of what was rightfully theirs. Geoff wasn't a Communist, not by any manner of means, but his teeth gritted angrily time and again when somebody promising left school for twenty-odd quid on the dole or a job filling supermarket shelves, just because the family needed the money. He nodded.

'Tell him!' shouted Spuggie.

'I don't need to tell him anything,' said Geoff. 'Except I'm proud of him and so should you be an' all.'

There wasn't anything else he could say. He couldn't manufacture anything, couldn't make things happen. And he didn't have a magic wand.

'It'll sort itself out,' said Geoff, 'in the fullness of time.' He was apt, in moments of stress, to use a slightly old-fashioned phrase and Fraser raised his eyebrows. Spuggie giggled and Geoff smiled to himself as he walked off. It would sort itself out.

Across the other side of town, some more sorting out was going on. Brad and Alison were 'seeing each other', as it was termed. And things had firmed up between them to the extent that Brad was at this very moment peeling a 'For Sale' sign out of the window of the modest little terraced house he and Alison were about to turn into an ideal home. It was Alison's idea to get somewhere cheap and do it up before they got married. Brad grimaced a little. Most of what he found himself doing these days turned out to stem from an idea of Alison's. He was very fond of her but, just occasionally, a rising tide of panic would well up from the pit of his stomach at the sheer speed of events. It didn't seem like a minute since he had first fancied her and asked her out and courted her with a stubborn determination which had finally put paid to his only rival, the lovely Mike.

And now they had bought a house and an old Turkish proverb his father used to quote sprang into his mind. 'When the house is built,' his father used to intone solemnly. 'When the house is built, the man dies!' Life was a galloping horse these days, and Brad clung frantically to its tail as it tugged down the precipice to married bliss. Then Alison leaned behind him, pushing all her softness into his back and blowing gently on his neck, and he thought to himself that maybe

Turkish sayings were a load of old cobblers anyway. He frowned and rubbed the window, suddenly seeing somebody across the street, walking slowly, head down; somebody he had never expected to see in Newcastle upon Tyne again.

'What?' said Alison curiously, rubbing slowly against his back and making him tingle. He shook his head, not wanting to disturb the moment. But he was absolutely certain that he had seen little Julie once more after all these months.

He had. She was going across town to where she had lived with her father after he and her mother had split up. The telephone was never answered these days. Julie was going to see if her dad was still there but, as she let herself into the cold house, she realised he hadn't been for some considerable time. She telephoned her mum, looking round the loveless room, and promised she would come home the following day. Then she set out to have one last look at the town and maybe meet some friends from the old days.

By coincidence, down at the Grove, word had got round that Julie was back in town and this had naturally enough stirred up thoughts of Gill's death. Donna, who had fallen out with Nicola over Jan, was reduced to talking to Debbie Dobson and Jemma about the tragedy. She began by saying she thought Gill's death had been really romantic, almost like James Dean. But Debbie got right to the point.

'I thought you couldn't stand Gillespie,' she said.

Jemma told her to shut up, wanting Donna to tell them more, but then the lads arrived, mob-handed as usual.

P.J. was bursting with his latest scheme which was to be the best magician in the world. He was going to need an assistant, though, in fishnet tights. Donna said she'd sooner be the meat in a lad sandwich which set the lads off, roaring and punching each other as they went.

Jemma thought about what Donna had said. 'What's a lad

sandwich?' she asked and had scorn poured over her by Debbie, who didn't know either but wasn't going to admit it. Donna's admirers were interrupted by their sister Nicola with the bad news that their dad was at the end of the lane with the van and if they didn't go shopping for new shoes right now, they would be dead, Saturday or not. They grumbled but went.

Nicola nodded coolly at Donna and turned to go. Donna breathed deeply and, without actually meaning to, asked, 'What are you doing with yourself these days?' After quite a long pause, Nicola turned and looked at her.

'Not a lot,' she said.

Donna had come this far and felt she might just as well get on with it. 'You still seeing that Paul, out the Light Brigade? You want to be careful with him, you know.' Nicola grinned. 'I tell you what,' said Donna. 'If you promise not to slap me face, I'll let you come down the Metro Centre with us, tonight.' Then they both grinned and it was as if they had never been apart. They knew the slap had been both given and deserved and would now be forgotten. They collapsed in giggles with their arms round each other. Then they looked up at the sound of Julie's voice, sad and soft. 'Hello, Nicola. Hello, Donna.' They put their arms round her and they all sat together and talked about old times.

Geoff and Mary O'Malley watched them from the window. Mary said she was surprised that Julie had come back now and not when Gill was buried. Geoff snapped at her and she shut up, not knowing what was wrong but not liking it either.

The hooting, roaring bunch of lads had finally settled in the games room, still jostling and pushing, as lads do, but talking seriously at the same time about P.J.'s idea. They showed Fraser P.J.'s book about magic and Fraser shook his head. 'Nae chance,' was his considered opinion. But P.J. persisted. He knew his idea of doing a magic show would do

15

his all-round reputation as an entertainer no harm at all – he was looking for a mega illusion and an occasion to perform it. Duncan thought a record-breaking stunt like sawing twenty girls in half all at the same time was a good idea. And Speedy had heard of a bloke at the British Legion who took women's bras off without them feeling a thing. They looked at him till he shut up and then Sobersides Fraser had the best idea of all.

'Do something for charity,' he said. 'Then Geoff'll be bound to give you a hand.' P.J. nodded. This was definitely a bonny plan. And Speedy made it better by suggesting that the best charity would be Robert's physiotherapy place which needed equipment. The others nodded.

'How's Robert doing, anyway?' P.J. asked.

Speedy told them his friend was nearly as good as new and would be flying down the wing with the best of them in a couple of weeks, maybe even playing for the town again in a month.

Speedy, as usual, had not got it quite right. Robert was having difficulty walking, let alone playing anything, and was growing extremely touchy about the whole business. Until now he had just assumed that as soon as he'd got rid of his crutches everything would be back to normal. He would be just the same as he had always been. Over at Lou and Nick's, he struggled across the kitchen and Lou watched him anxiously. Joanne came in to say that Charley was on the telephone and wanted to know if it was all right to come over.

'Tell her I'm busy,' said Robert, banging his fist on his thigh in frustration.

'What?' said Lou, when Joanne had gone back to the telephone. He didn't think he was much of a boyfriend was the problem and he said so. Lou tried to reason him out of his blackness but there was no way and so she left, being wise in the ways of young people growing up.

At the Grove the three girls sat and chattered and Julie remembered all the good things about Newcastle. Then she fell silent and Nicola put her hand on her knee.

'Don't blame yourself,' Nicola said. 'It wasn't your fault.'

But Julie was far away, almost talking to herself. 'It's funny,' she mused. 'Sometimes I can't even remember his face. Sometimes I think he's just gone out of the room.'

Donna immediately put her foot in it by asking Julie for a photograph of Gill. Nicola went hot and cold as Julie looked at Donna in disbelief. Gill and Donna had mixed about as well as oil and water. They'd always hated each other. Nicola gave her tactless mate a look that could have boiled soup. She turned to Julie.

'Take no notice of her. She thinks it's romantic, Gill dying.'

Julie turned her eyes sombrely on Donna and told her slowly and carefully how long it had taken Gill to die, just how badly he'd been damaged, every bone below his waist smashed. And then she wept as she said the last few words. 'It was a blessing he did die. But it wasn't romantic. He won't see the sun again or feel the wind on his face. Or the rain in his hair. And he'll never bounce a baby on his knee. Never bounce his baby on his knee.' And she cried to herself. Because she knew, deep down inside, no matter what, that she wished she'd never gone away. Donna and Nicola put their arms round her and held her while she shook.

The next day was chaos in the Dobson household. This wasn't unusual. Every day was chaos in the Dobson household, at least for the first hour, while everybody stole everybody else's tights and quarrelled about who was next in the bathroom. When the dust finally settled and they all started to walk to school, Debbie was still furious because she was convinced that Jemma's fat stupid legs were being protected from the weather by a pair of Debbie's new lacy tights. Jemma walked faster and faster, trying to catch up with Nicola for protection. She didn't like the look on Debbie's face and she didn't relish the thought of having her tights ripped off in front of a bus stop full of grinning lads. She knew she had nice legs but she could think of better ways of showing them off. She swore a bit under her breath, though, when she saw that her big sister was standing simpering at the Prince of Whales, the Jolly Green Brigadier himself, Mr Bighead Paul Skerrett with the loopy earring and the mountain bike.

'Come on, Nick,' said Jemma hopefully. 'We'll miss the bus.'

It wouldn't have mattered if she'd told Nicola that she'd forgotten to put her jeans on and was standing in her knickers in front of the whole of Newcastle.

Paul grinned at Nicola. 'Hello, stranger,' he said and her answering grin was so broad she thought her face might crack.

'Hello,' she said, and cursed inwardly as she felt the telltale red flush make its way all over her face.

'There's something I'd like to talk to you about, if you've got a minute?' She nodded and waited.

By this time Debbie had caught up with Jemma. 'Right,' said Debbie. 'Take those tights off!'

Jemma distracted her by pointing out the two lovebirds, who were actually standing so close they were touching in some places. Jemma said she thought he was creepy and Debbie nodded as they watched developments, eyes wide.

Paul gripped Nicola by the shoulders. 'He's going to kiss

her in the street right in front of everybody,' said Jemma, mouth open.

Debbie nodded. 'I don't believe it,' she said. 'Not in the street. Not this time of the morning.' But he did. He kissed her right on the mouth (to a chorus of hoots and jeers from the bus stop), and gave her a piece of paper. She looked at the address on it as he pedalled off, shouting that he'd meet her at half-past eight that very night.

Jemma and Debbie rushed up, agog. But she looked straight through them. Her eyes were sparkling and there was a lovely warm feeling in her stomach. Paul had kissed her properly for the first time and had looked deep into her eyes as he did it. And tonight she was going to see him again. Jemma looked after her and shook her head. There would be tears before bedtime in her opinion. She noticed Debbie looking at the tights again and spoke hastily.

'Do you think we should tell me mam about that lad?' she said.

Debbie looked at her. 'If you get a hole in those tights, I'll pull all your hair out.'

'OK,' said Jemma obligingly. 'It's a deal.' She knew Debbie never fulfilled any of her threats. And she really did look good in the lacy tights.

The young people of Newcastle are pretty much the same as young people anywhere. They go to school, most of them, moaning on the way. Some go in, get their names recorded and then spend the rest of the day complaining that there isn't anything to do. There are very few children who hurry to school. Some do, if it's raining, and that's about it. Robert would have liked to be able to hurry to school. Instead he was heaving his almost useless legs one after the other, while Speedy followed with the wheelchair, looking at his watch and finally exploding with frustration.

'You canna walk all the way to school,' observed Speedy, circling with the wheelchair, as Robert struggled for all the world like a beleaguered wagon train. Robert grunted back that he'd walk until he could walk no more and only then would he get in the cripple wagon, and that he would decide when, and if Speedy didn't like it, he could put it where the monkey put the nuts. Speedy began arguing, which is one of the things Speedy is best at, and Lou came piling down the path to break it up. She took one look at Robert's angry, sad face and jerked her head at Speedy who knew better than to argue any more and disappeared.

Lou Gallagher kneeled down in front of Robert. 'Right, you,' she said.

Robert looked away. He knew he was being unreasonable but all he wanted was to be left alone to find out for himself how much was left of the old Robert from before his neck had taken those sickening cracks. He told Lou slowly and sadly and she nodded.

'Maybe,' she said. 'Maybe, Robert, but how many others are you going to smash to pieces while you find out about yourself?'

Robert looked down again. 'I don't know what you mean,' he protested but Lou shook her head. They both knew what she meant. She meant that he had all but broken Charley's heart. He hadn't spoken to her for more than a week, he'd refused to see her when she came to the house, he wouldn't talk to her on the telephone. His voice, when he finally replied, was husky.

'She's better off without me,' he muttered.

Lou flashed back at him without thinking. 'You should let Charley be the judge of that! You can't take it all on yourself! You're not God!' she exclaimed.

He grinned wryly. 'If I was,' he said, 'I would make some changes.' And he looked down at his wobbly legs. But there was no time to finish speaking because Joanne came out of the house with her mouth set and her eyes like thunder. She gave Lou the letter from the immigration place where her brother was waiting for permission to join her after escaping from the hopeless poverty of Vietnam.

Lou had seen the letter arrive earlier and her heart had sunk. The authorities were taking a very long time over what had originally seemed quite straightforward. Brother and sister needed to be together, Lou reasoned. But the men in suits had doubts. When Lou tried to hurry things up a little, she received a very frosty reply. The man she had spoken to on the telephone had said that the boy writing to Joanna and claiming to be her brother had a good deal to prove before he would be allowed into the country.

Joanne waved the letter again. 'I don't understand,' she said. 'Why don't they just tell us where he is and then you could go down and sort it out?'

Lou looked at the little troubled face and put her arm round Joanne's shoulders. 'We'll sort it out, pet. Tonight. After I come back with Robert from the physio.' And she looked at Robert determinedly making his way down the street and she sighed again. She wasn't looking forward to visiting the physio. No matter how many kind noises people made, Lou knew enough to make her own mind up. She didn't think Robert would ever run for a bus again, never mind play football for England. Somebody would have to tell him soon and he would have to find himself a new aim in life.

Back at the Grove, Geoff and Alison were looking at a sour-faced Brad who was lining them up for a photograph. They were arguing at the same time about a memorial for Gill. Geoff thought it was wrong that there wasn't even a marker on his grave. But Alison didn't think they should encourage the kids to be morbid.

'I'm right!' she said.

Brad packed his camera away. 'There's a coincidence,' he muttered. 'That's the fourteenth time you've been right this week and it's still only Monday.'

Geoff and Alison looked at each other as Brad marched stiffly to his car, stuffing his equipment in noisily and leaving with a harsh rev of his engine and a clatter of gears. She shook her head and Geoff was glad enough to let it lie.

'It's all right wanting to remember Gill,' she urged. 'That's all right. Only let it be something that isn't a gravestone.'

He looked at her, suddenly realising what she meant.

'Aye. That's right,' said Alison. 'Winston's put Gill's name on the grave, picked out in little stones. Who's going to tell him that's not good enough?'

Geoff was silent, remembering Winston's icy little face as the coffin had gone into the ground.

At the back end of the afternoon, Lou and Robert sat in the doctor's office. She had intercepted them on the way into the gym. They stared at the fuzzy bones outlined on the X-ray screen as the sun shone through the slats of the venetian blind and the little dots of dust danced in the beams. Robert listened sullenly, refusing to believe what was being said. Then he got up slowly and painfully. Lou and the doctor watched. In the silence, his words fell like stones.

'You're wrong,' said Robert. 'I'll play. You'll see.' He dragged himself out, supporting his weight with the stick.

He was slowly limping up the drive to the Grove when he felt a light tap on the back of his arm. He turned to see Charley, smiling at him hopefully. The smile died when she saw his face, grim and bitter. She hesitated, then blurted it out.

'I haven't seen you for so long. Don't you want anything to

do with me any more?' He didn't say anything and her heart sank. 'I have to know,' she persisted.

He looked at her and she began to hope a little. His deep brown eyes were the same ones she had drowned in a mere couple of months ago. He looked at the ground and she had to strain to hear him.

'Maybe it'll be better if we don't see each other for a bit,' he murmured and she felt as if she had been hit with a bar of iron. She turned quickly before the hot tears could force themselves out. Then she marched down the drive, head high, dying inside, and he watched her go, wishing he could call her back, knowing there was no future for them while he had nothing to give her.

The day drew to a close. Inspired by a chat from Geoff about the need for a memorial for Gill, the Fabulous Five (P.J., Fraser, Speedy, Winston and Duncan) had gone over to the magic shop in Backleigh to suss out the chances of putting on a mega magic show to raise money.

The shop, when they found it at the bottom of a dark little street, was closed. But there were still some little red lights on which made it look rather like a mouth, although nobody liked to say so for fear of being teased by the others.

As they looked in the window, one by one, they noticed a skull which slowly opened and closed its mouth. Its eyes began to glow red and it somehow seemed to be getting closer. When a skeletal arm lifted and beckoned to them, the boys thought maybe it was time they did certain other things. They didn't quite run but they didn't walk slowly either.

Meanwhile Julie needed cheering up, so she wandered down to the Metro Centre with Donna. As ever, the sheer flash and warmth and happiness of the place enchanted her, and she soaked up the well-remembered North-Eastern tones, so far removed from the pinched gentility of where she lived now. Donna told her the scandalous tale of how she had pretended that she and Jan had, to coin a phrase, gone all the way. And Julie giggled in spite of herself when Donna described the smack round the ear she had had off Nicola for doing it. Then, while they were still hooting with laughter, Nicola herself arrived, walking on air after her date with Paul. Her face was pink and her eyes were sparkling.

Donna looked at her and remarked drily that she looked as if she'd been moving the earth, not saving it. Nicola blushed and Donna elbowed Julie.

'Stop it, Donna!' said Nicola but she obviously wanted to tell them all about her evening with Paul's friends in the plushiest house she had ever been in. They had treated her as if she was quite grown up and listened to her ideas with patience and understanding, even when she had let her head run faster than her tongue could catch up with.

She didn't tell them about her walk from the bus in the dark with Paul where she had been treated as if she was grown up too – a different kind of grown up – and parts of her were still tingling from it. But she didn't need to tell Donna. The signs were all there anyway.

Julie stayed with them all evening, finally saying goodbye and climbing up the hill to the cold, empty house where she would only spend one more night before going to get on with the rest of her life. She made a cup of tea and sat down with it, jumping up suddenly when the doorbell rang.

At the door, she had the shock of her life. Carl stood there, lopsided sneer in place, a cigarette hanging from the corner of his mouth.

'Couldn't keep away, then?' he said.

Julie had never been able to cope with Carl. Her hand tightened nervously at the collar of her dressing gown as he looked pointedly at the lace top of her nightie. He grinned at her again as she stepped back.

'What do you want, Carl?' she asked. 'At this time of night?'

He stepped into the doorway.

'If you let us in,' he said, 'I'll tell you.'

CHAPTER TWO

Geoff is famous for worrying and his latest worry was double-headed. He was worrying about Fraser whose undoubted talent was about to be chucked down the wastepaper basket just to earn a bob or two, and he was worrying in a less defined way about Alison. If you had told him he was at all concerned about Alison he would have been very surprised. She and Brad fitted together like bacon and eggs, and yet there was something about the way her lips tightened after one of Brad's sallies and the slight crinkle in her brow which seemed to be permanent these days that made Geoff stop and think from time to time. So he chuntered round the building and worried about leaking roofs and smashed windows and time and again his worries were drawn back to Fraser and Alison. He didn't worry about Brad and later on, when the dust had settled, he knew that this was because Brad was a survivor.

Nicola lay awake half the night and thought about Paul. When she wasn't thinking about Paul, she was thinking about herself with Paul and how much she was falling in love with him. She shivered with delight in the warm snugness of her bed. If Geoff had only known, he would have been much better employed worrying about Nicola. But what the eye doesn't see the heart doesn't grieve over, as Mary O'Malley was heard to intone on many an occasion.

So Nicola's eyes were just a bit heavy the next morning and her mind was far away, as she blundered out of the gate and straight into Paul and a brief but exciting nuzzle.

'Off to school?' asked Paul and the naughty twinkle in his eye was as bright as the glint of his earring.

She was pert with her answer. 'Unless I get a better offer,' she said, and he bent closer and whispered his warm breath into her ear.

She recoiled, open-mouthed. 'What?' she exclaimed, her face brightening and blushing all at the same time, and he grinned at the confusion he had caused.

He raised his eyebrows. 'Surely, you don't want me shouting it all over the street?' he said, and opened his mouth as if he was going to, until she shook her head quickly.

'Straight from school, then, OK? I'll pick you up at the Grove.'

And before she knew where she was, he was gone and she could still feel his warm breath on her cheek and the slight wetness of him on her lips. She went to school but she might just as well have gone to the moon for all the attention anybody got.

Debbie and Jemma had been watching the whole business from behind the hedge at the end of the road. Now they debated whether or not to tell their mother that it looked as if she might be a grandmother soon. Like most little girls, they had fairly lurid imaginations but in the end they decided to keep quiet about it. After all, if Nicola did run off with Paul, one of them would get a bigger bedroom and the other one could have the pick of her wardrobe. Practical considerations won the day.

Julie got up later than she would have liked and, thinking about what had happened the night before, shook her head in disbelief. Carl had wanted to come in but had then seen that she was scared of him. He'd backed away like a little boy, outraged that she had got the wrong idea.

She made her way slowly to the squat where she and Gill had lived for such a short, happy time. Everything was just the same as she had left it, even the ginger cat delicately stepping off the wall and arching its back with a hoarse rasp of greeting. She pushed open the creaky gate and went into the house and up the stairs, seeing Gill all around her but

27

distant and only half remembered, as if it had all happened to somebody else.

Carl was sitting on the bed, head down, strangely diffident when she went into the room. He lived there now and all the posters on the walls were different – martial arts and kung fu and pictures of soldiers and bulging muscles. He saw her looking and smiled quietly. 'Different interests,' he said and she nodded. He talked around things for a while, gradually building up to what he really wanted to say. She could see what he was doing and realised that Carl, the neighbourhood thug, was shy. She shook her head slightly, wondering, and he caught the movement and blurted out suddenly, 'It was my fault. I caused it. Me and Gillespie never got on.'

His voice grew gruffer as he went on. 'I said I was going to the police after that bump he had with the motor, if he didn't cough up some cash. I knew he never had any cash, I just wanted to make him sweat a bit, like.'

He looked up and saw the horror in her eyes and felt ashamed but glad, too, in a funny way. He didn't want her to think that it had been her fault because it hadn't. It had been his.

Julie bit her lip, thinking. It had been all their faults, really. Hers and Winston's and Carl's. Then she thought again and realised that it had been Gill's fault most of all. The thought didn't make her feel much better.

Then Carl surprised her even more. He took Gill's leather jacket out of the big cupboard and gave it to her. She didn't know what to say but just stood there cradling it.

'They sent his things back here,' said Carl almost apologetically. 'I was going to give it that little runt, Winston, and then they said you'd come back. You owe us six quid.'

She looked at him in surprise until he explained that he'd had the jacket cleaned and looked down and she knew what had been cleaned off it and held it all the more tightly after she had given him the money.

Then she walked off down the street with it, the cool breeze tapping the side of her face, Newcastle upon Tyne laid out in front of her, with just one more thing to do before she left for ever. She was going to Fraser's school to see if she could get a word with him through the fence. Geoff had told her about Fraser's dilemma; how he would have to give up his studies and go to work because Spuggie and his mother needed the money. Julie had something to say about that. She had first-hand experience of a similar situation. And if Fraser wanted to do the right thing by everybody, he had to realise that there was somebody else who mattered too.

She was lucky. Fraser was there. Fraser was much luckier, being there to hear what Julie had to say. She pulled him over to one side, ignoring the glances and the wolf whistles. At first he only listened to be polite. Slowly, though, as the sense and the enormity of what she was saying sank in, he started to pay a good deal of attention. When she had finished, she put a soft hand on the back of his neck, stood on tiptoe and kissed Fraser and Newcastle goodbye. Fraser stood and watched her go, Gill's jacket clutched tight to her heart, and he knew Julie Warner had more guts and bottle than any of them had ever realised. He banged his fist into the palm of his hand and vowed to himself that if she could do it, so could he. Then he got his bike out of the bike shed and rode off into the wind. Just for today, school could take care of itself. He had things to work out. All the while he was riding, though, he thought of Julie and once, to his absolute horror, he found a little tear had fought its way out of his eye and a lump had somehow found its way into his throat.

On the train that rattled its way slowly over the empty river, Julie sat in Gill's jacket and looked at the photograph of her mother and herself and her baby Gillian, the baby Gill would never see. She didn't cry – she had cried herself dry. She took out her only photograph of Gill and held the two pictures side by side. Life was for living and one day she would be able to tell her daughter all about the wonderful boy who had been her father, about his sudden quick smile and his deep black moods and the smell of him and the way he had lightened her days for just a little while. Then she put the pictures away and started to catch up with her school work. A-levels were hard enough. A-levels and night feeds were something else again.

Fraser found Spuggie at the Grove with Joanne, and told her the good news about going on to get his A-levels. She told him his mind changed like the wind. He shook his head.

'I've just met someone that's had the same kind of problems as me,' he said. 'That's all. I've been persuaded.'

Spuggie rolled her eyes at Joanne. They were both going through a very silly phase and tended to laugh at almost everything. Then Fraser got cross and Spuggie immediately stopped laughing. She laid her hand on his arm and told him how fantastic it was and he nodded gruffly.

'It's all very well,' he said, 'but if you don't get qualifications, you've got no chance of looking after yourself, never mind anybody else.'

Spuggie was about to retort that she didn't need looking after, thanks very much, but Joanne caught her eye and she shut up.

Outside the Grove, Paul was standing a little way off, watching the kids scurrying to and fro. He'd heard a lot about Byker Grove and, from what he'd heard, it seemed like a good place to do a little advertising. Paul was in the ecology business to an almost fanatical degree and his one and only priority was saving the planet. He wanted to get as many people as possible on board his particular Ark, and he knew from past experience that the younger they were, the easier they were to recruit. What he didn't know was that Geoff always kept a weather eye out for what was happening at the

30

Grove. Now Geoff called Brad over to the window from which he had been watching Paul. Brad shook his head but then squinted a bit harder and nodded.

'Right,' said Brad. 'It's that lad Nicola Dobson's been hanging round with. Whatsisname, Paul something, I don't know.'

Geoff looked at Paul. Even from that distance there was something odd about him. The way he stood, possibly, and the watchful air put Geoff in mind of a kestrel looking at its lunch and he suddenly felt a little uneasy. He sent Brad down to invite Paul in – Geoff was never too sure of people who stood around and watched kids. While he was waiting, there was a knock at the office door and Fraser stood in the doorway, looking different somehow, more determined. He rattled out his new decision, about carrying on at school, and Geoff congratulated him, genuinely pleased. Fraser stood there after his little speech and looked at Geoff hopefully. Geoff was puzzled but not for long.

'I just wondered,' Fraser hesitated.

Geoff told him not to wonder but to ask and was a little taken aback when Fraser asked him for a job. Gwen had left under a cloud but Brad had as good as taken over as part-time helper, and the way funds were running out, Geoff only hoped he'd have a job himself at the end of the day. But he promised to keep an eye out and Fraser left, satisfied that Geoff was on his side.

Then Brad came back in and, to Geoff's amazement, hopped from foot to foot and asked Geoff if he could rely on him for a reference, should he need one. He also left Geoff with a nasty taste in his mouth, asking him not to say anything about it to Alison.

Geoff went down to the games room, thanking the Lord once again that he had broad shoulders, to find Paul with his feet firmly under the table, talking to an entranced bunch of Byker Grovers. Paul was personable and persuasive and,

31

close to, looked a lot more acceptable than he had from the window.

Geoff drew near and was rewarded with one of Paul's most disarming grins. Despite himself, Geoff smiled back.

'I'm just on my hobby horse,' said Paul. 'Telling this lot how important it is to save the world for the people that are yet to be born. I'm an ecology freak. I wondered if you'd mind me coming down now and again and giving a bit of a talk?'

Geoff grinned again. 'If you can get this lot interested in saving anything, I'll give you free tea for a month,' and the deal was struck. It was P.J.'s turn to claim Geoff's time and the session was over, anyway.

Nicola arrived with Charley and took possession of Paul's right arm. 'What are you doing with this lot?' she asked pointedly, and when he told her he was converting them, she said tartly that he hadn't finished converting her yet. Then he whispered in her ear and that stopped her chatter and made her look at all the little kids who were watching with frank and undisguised nosiness. He let her pull him away, smiling all the while, and Charley watched them go. Their obvious delight in each other did nothing to ease the pain in the pit of her stomach. The songs always seemed to get it wrong when they talked about love being to do with the heart. With Charley, it always went straight to her belly. It stayed there, too. She shook her head, impatient with herself, and went to find someone to talk to.

In the office, P.J. was in full flow, trying to persuade Geoff to finance a magic show, with himself as star, in order to raise money for a memorial to Gill. They only needed ten pounds, they said. When they came out, they needed nine. As Geoff put it, all they had to do was find another nine mugs and they were in business. Duncan took charge of the pound and noted it down carefully in his accounts book – 'received: one pound'.

Winston had his own ideas about memorials. Gill would get the best gravestone money could buy as soon as the funds could be raised. Until then, there would be fresh flowers, even if sometimes they were only daisies or buttercups. Kelly privately believed that Winston spent too much time thinking about his dead friend, but most of the time she kept him company, always looking for the chance to bring a smile to his face. She said she'd go over to the churchyard with him if they could all go round to the Dobsons afterwards and watch a video. Jemma had recently decided to cure Debbie's terror of anything remotely ghostly by exposing her to as many horror movies as they could con out of the video shop man. She also thought it might be a good idea for Debbie to walk over some dead people from time to time, to prove that skeletal hands didn't claw up through the ground to grab little ankles. Debbie tossed her head, saying she wasn't scared and that was that.

But when they got there, even Jemma had to admit that the graveyard was just a shade spooky. The light was fading and the rooks were settling down for the evening as the wind whistled through the tall trees and hissed through the tombstones, rattling the grass and making Winston's job of filling the vase harder than it should have been. He did it, finally, and stepped back to admire his work. The girls instinctively moved a little closer to him and Debbie thought for a moment of suggesting that they should say a prayer or something. Kelly looked at Winston's small face, still full of loss, and a great wave of motherliness swept over her. She was just about to put her arm round him when a huge great lolloping dog bounced right across the grave and scattered the flowers, pebbles, vase and all in several directions. Then it sat on the bare ground and grinned at them with its tongue hanging out and its tail wagging furiously.

Winston looked round wildly for something to throw at it but Kelly went right up and grabbed the trailing piece of string attached to its collar. The dog fell silent at once and sat by Kelly obediently. It was the kind of dog she'd often seen at home in the country before they moved, a greyhound retriever cross, a lurcher, a poacher's dog, fast across the ground to catch rabbits and hares and whatever else would go in a poacher's stew.

'It's a lurcher,' Kelly said, while the others repaired the damage it had done. 'Poacher's dog!' She ruffled its ears and it grinned delightedly.

'It'll get run over round here,' Winston said grimly and it didn't sound as if he'd be too sorry if it did. The girls shot a reproachful look at him.

He had a sudden thought. Maybe the dog had come from the travellers' camp, the tinkers who were squatting at Backleigh. There might be a reward as well and he told the others they should take it back. Debbie looked at him darkly and chanted, soon followed by the others, the rhyme they had all known since mixed infants. 'My mother said, I never should, play with the gypsies in the wood!'

But they took as little notice of folk rhymes as they did of school noticeboards and off they set, with the dog bouncing along happily in front of them, a real urchin of a dog, smelling all the interesting new smells and cocking his leg whenever he could. Jemma looked at him every time he did it with fascinated horror.

'Why do they do that?' she asked finally.

'Marking their territory,' said Kelly.

'But why?' Jemma persisted. 'Human beings don't. Why should dogs?'

Winston was feeling better and better. It was because he had something to do, of course, rather than moping and moaning and thinking about Gill, but it made him crack a joke for the first time in months.

'Human beings don't need to,' he piped. 'They nip down to Texas Homecare and buy some new wallpaper.'

This tickled Debbie's funny bone and she giggled all the way to the edge of the woods with Jemma, who had the feeling the joke was on her for once, telling her to shut up. Once they were in the woods, though, they didn't feel quite so chirpy. The trees seemed to lean over the four of them as they walked along. Debbie stopped giggling, Jemma stopped ticking her off, and Kelly leaned closer to Winston, while the dog seemed to take on a new sense of purpose. He knew all these smells and this was his territory so no leg-cocking was required. He pulled hard on the string, tugging them faster and faster until with a burst they were in a clearing surrounded by vans, those vans beloved of travelling people, faintly raffish, with chrome and fancy curtains but with a vaguely menacing air like pirate ships at anchor in a sleepy fishing port. There was nobody about.

The dog led them at a fast clip towards the only van which didn't seem to fit in. It was a truly old gypsy caravan with a little chimney and a back step and faded paintwork with whirls and curlicues and little prancing figures painted all over it. Over the door, there was a sign. Jemma read it out, having appointed herself the official spokesperson. 'Sister Tabitha,' she read. 'Fortunes told.' A deep voice from behind made them jump and turn and stare, their hearts beating like a collective trip hammer. A deeply tanned and smiling woman stood there, with a strange elfin boy peeping from behind her skirts.

'What have we here?' she said. 'Here's a fine band of pilgrims come to see us, Paget.'

And she brought the little elf out in front of her. His wide eyes fixed on them as if they were from another planet, with their brightly coloured shell suits and trainers.

Winston offered up the dog on the string rather like a missionary with a set of beads, and she took the hound and tied it to the post at the side of the caravan. One after the other, they told the tale, each one taking it up as the one before ran out of steam or faltered in the light of Tabitha's understanding smile. She nodded as Winston finished.

'He knocked over some flowers on a grave,' he said sadly.

Tabitha smiled again. 'Grave robbers, are you?' she asked. 'I can hardly believe that, bright-faced innocents like you? No, surely?'

They started to stammer and explain but soon realised she was only joking. She gave them a sprig of heather to put on the grave and shooed them off, making them hurry a little with her last remark.

'Get away,' she warned, 'before the men get nigh. They eat little 'uns like you on toast.'

And so they shot off, knowing, of course, that she was joking but not wanting to take any unnecessary chances.

Winston was quieter on the way back. Several times Jemma or Kelly tried to get him to talk but his mind was on Tabitha's van. 'Fortunes told,' it had said. But she had also given them heather and had told them to put it on their friend's grave. He shook his head. How had she known it was a friend? And if she could tell fortunes, maybe she could tell other things too. Maybe she could even tell him where Gill was now. It was lucky Kelly didn't know what he was thinking. But she was glad enough to be away from the camp and out of the woods.

While all this had been going on, a drama of a different kind had been playing itself out in an ordinary little house on the other side of Backleigh. Joanne had been playing a skipping game with Spuggie, her thoughts far away for once from long-lost brothers and fatherless little girls and dead mothers, all of which usually occupied far too many of her waking hours. In Lou's opinion, watching out of her kitchen window, Spuggie's arrival at the foster home had been the making of Joanne. Her usual icy reserve and controlled

36

manner had melted in the face of flame-haired Spuggie's fire and wit. Spuggie, without actually being aware of it, had set out to turn Joanne into a little girl again and, watching them skip, Lou could see what a good job she was doing. Lou smiled as Joanne jumped and hooted and giggled while Spuggie swung the rope faster and faster.

She hardly heard the telephone ring, she was so engrossed. And when she finally did pick it up, she was still so lost in her own thoughts that it took her a little while to realise who was calling. It was Mr Hayward, the solicitor who had been helping them with Joanne's brother's immigration problems.

'I'm sorry, Mrs Gallagher,' he said. 'It's bad news.'

Lou listened with mounting dread as he carried on and then, when he had finished, replaced the telephone numbly. Her face was white as she passed the mirror in the hall. 'Oh, the poor pet,' she muttered. 'The poor pet.' And she stood in the doorway and called to Joanne, knowing that she was going to destroy her hopes and her future.

Joanne skipped in, face flushed and happy. She took one look at Lou and immediately put her hands over her ears. 'Don't tell me,' she shrieked. 'Don't tell me! I don't want to know!' She fled up the stairs to the bedroom.

Spuggie looked at Lou, and Lou shook her head. 'I'm going to need some of your courage, Spuggie,' she said eventually, and Spuggie nodded. She knew it had to do with Joanne's brother.

Lou went upstairs with a heavy heart, and found the little girl spread out across the bed. She had taken all the letters her brother had written and flung them across the room. Lou sat down and put her arm round her and sensibly told the whole story without patronising her by trying to hide anything. Growing up isn't easy. It is made much harder when grown-ups tell children lies and so Lou told Joanne that the young man who had been writing to her for so long was a fake and not her brother. He had a set of forged papers and had been trying to use Joanne to get into the country. The immigration authorities had finally tricked him into telling the truth and Mr Hayward had been told to let Joanne know.

After a while, she stopped crying and sat up and looked at Lou.

'Why?' she asked. 'Why would anybody do that to me?'

Lou had no comfort to give, so Joanne looked at all the letters scattered on the floor. She picked them up and went into the garden and burned them all in the litter bin. Spuggie and Lou watched her, knowing that she was setting fire to her hopes and dreams.

When Fraser came home a little later they told him the story. He didn't say anything but his face took on the thoughtful cast they had all come to know so well. As she watched him, for no reason she could think of, Lou suddenly felt a little more hopeful.

Then Joanne put the matter right out of her mind and took Spuggie off down to the Grove where they got heavily involved in some nonsense with P.J., Jemma and Debbie. Jemma had just caused Debbie the biggest embarrassment of her young life (at least as bad as the time her skirt fell off in mixed PE). Jemma had told P.J. that DEBBIE KEPT HIS PHOTOGRAPH ON THE WALL OF HER BEDROOM! Debbie changed colour as fast as a firework and felt the sweat dripping down the middle of her back. But P.J. is essentially a nice guy. He could see what Debbie was going through and, almost without thinking, asked her for a photograph for *his* bedroom wall. Jemma nearly gagged. Debbie's eyes shone. Speedy whooped.

P.J. looked down at Debbie's face, full of hero-worship and schoolgirl lust, and thought that maybe for once his silver tongue had really got him into trouble. Then he looked at her again and the thought spread around the back of his mind that Debbie actually had quite a nice smile. He felt his own silly smile growing broader and gruffly suggested that they should go and have a committee meeting or something.

In the office, Lou had rung Geoff about Joanne's problems. Geoff promised to keep an eye out for her, put the telephone down, and groaned quietly to himself. Problems, problems, problems. He lifted his head as Fraser came into the office, looking thoughtful. Geoff waited apprehensively.

'Geoff,' said Fraser. 'You know Joanne's had a bit of a knock with that brother business, don't you?' Geoff nodded.

'Suppose she traced her father, the American?' Fraser went on.

'How would she do that?' said Geoff cautiously, and Fraser sat down and expanded a little on how various things might be made to happen. Geoff listened and, once again aware of Fraser's intelligence, looked at him with affection and a little bit of awe. Whatever Fraser wanted to do in life, Geoff thought, he was going to be very good at it.

'What do you want me to do?' he asked. Fraser shook his head.

'I just wanted to try it out on you, that's all,' the lad replied and got to his feet. He went to the door and turned and grinned at Geoff who held a hand up in front of his face, fingers crossed to guard against vampires. 'What are you doing that for?' Fraser laughed, though he knew why Geoff was doing it.

'Because I'm just about to get conned into doing something, that's why,' replied Geoff.

Before he knew it, and despite the crossed fingers, he had agreed to give Fraser a lift down to the big library and the loan of the price of an airmail letter to the United States of America. Fraser reads the papers avidly, you see, and something he had noticed earlier in the week seemed to him to be the answer to everything that Joanne wanted out of life. Given a fair wind and a good crack of the whip, Fraser was about to do the mega good deed of the year.

Meanwhile, outside the Grove, a fierce argument was raging. Winston had become more morose than ever since their visit to the gypsy encampment and Kelly had finally reached the end of her tether.

'It's about time you got a grip on yourself,' she flared. 'You're just being morbid.'

Winston gave as good as he got, while the others stood listening in silent fascination. The fact was that Winston just wanted to tell someone how he felt. There wasn't anyone close enough, that was the problem. Looking at Kelly and P.J. and Duncan and Speedy, he realised they weren't really old enough. But he started anyway. 'I can't stop thinking about him, just because he's dead, can I?' he asked the silent group.

They looked at each other, embarrassed, and shifted from foot to foot. Young people aren't often encouraged to face their feelings these days and they don't often talk about them either. Winston looked at his friends, willing them to understand.

'If it was *your* best mate that had died, you would be thinking about it too! You would! Wouldn't you?' he said.

Kelly was cross at what she had started. She hadn't wanted to put Winston on the defensive and now she wanted desperately to let him off the hook. She knew he had been badly affected by Gill's death but he had to let go some time and the time to let go was now. She told him so, but he just looked at her and shook his head and marched away, lips set, teeth clenched, totally stubborn. He knew how he felt. If nobody else was prepared to listen then that was up to them. They watched him go and all felt a little ashamed, knowing that Winston needed something they weren't equipped to give him.

Duncan spoke first. Duncan was from a good, solid Roman Catholic family, perhaps one of the best religions in the world for dealing with death.

'He'll get over it,' he said, thinking privately that maybe he ought to have a word with Father Bennett, except that he didn't know what religion Winston was, if any.

Speedy kicked idly at a tussock of rough grass while offering his considered opinion. 'I'll tell you what,' he said. 'It's dead boring, all this harking on about Gill.' He warmed to his theme and spoke emphatically. 'If Gill was here now himself, he'd be the first one to tell Winston to shut up. He would!'

The others thought about it, and eventually Debbie looked round just as a cloud passed over the sun and a sudden twittering flight of starlings helped to darken the early evening sky.

'What do you mean,' asked Debbie, 'if Gill was here now? How could Gill be here now? He's dead.' The silence grew a little deeper.

'What if he is, though?' said Jemma. 'He spent enough time here. I wouldn't be surprised if he did come back to listen to what we're saying about him.'

It was only a coincidence, of course, that just at that moment a church bell started to toll long, ponderous notes, and a little breeze chilled the air and a cloud passed the setting sun which shone directly into the windows of the Grove. Two of those windows were pointed right at our little band of pilgrims who suddenly felt quite small and alone. The windows looked like two bright red eyes and Duncan stared hard at the next window along where somebody was looking out.

'Who's that?' he said quietly. 'Up there, at that window?'

They all turned round and looked. There was nobody there but Duncan insisted that there had been. They all looked at each other and by common consent decided there wasn't much point hanging round in the cold.

They went in and played table tennis. All of them, that is, except Debbie who ran home as fast as her legs would carry

41

her and got a photograph which didn't make her look quite as stupid as photos normally did and ran all the way back to where P.J. was playing Speedy for ten pence. He won and sat down. She sat down by him and gave him the photograph. She smiled hopefully.

'Is this one any good?' she asked. He grinned and put it in his inside pocket and she hugged herself with secret glee.

'I'm going to teach, you, Deborah,' he announced with panache, 'to be a magician's assistant.'

She nodded eagerly. She would have nodded if he had said he was going to teach her to eat concrete. Debbie had a crush on P.J.

Her sister had a crush on Paul. She was sitting alone with him on a grassy bank and listening adoringly to his view of the world. She agreed with everything he said, of course, even if some of it did sound a little impractical. For instance, she couldn't really see how they were going to stop people wanting to drive big cars, even though she understood that they were ripping holes in the ozone layer. Or was that the greenhouse effect? She wasn't quite sure and resolved to listen harder but it was pretty hard to concentrate when Paul's hand was stroking her neck in that particular way of his. And when he touched his tongue very gently to the middle of her ear, all pretence at concentrating went right out of the window and she glued her lips to his and kissed his socks off. When they came up for air, he grinned at her and her heart flipped again. He was saying something and she didn't quite catch it, but she nodded anyway.

It wasn't until she was thinking about him all over again late at night in bed that she realised she had agreed to meet him at five o'clock next Saturday, to do something about the ozone layer, or at any rate about people who drove big, fast, petrol-guzzling cars. She hugged her pillow and pretended it was him.

42

Brad's evening hadn't gone all that well. He had been think-ing that maybe he and Alison could drop the decorating materials off at the house, then maybe go and do something interesting, like a meal out or a drink or a game of pool or some bowling or a movie. Or almost anything, he thought wryly, that wasn't slapping paint on walls or nailing up cupboards or laying lino tiles or fitting new lavatory bowls.

He got to the house and whistled his signature tune, her favourite dance theme, so that she'd know he was coming. He might just as well have saved his breath to cool his porridge. Her car wasn't there, she wasn't there, and his dreams of a different kind of evening evaporated into the night. The only evidence that Alison had been anywhere near was the message painted neatly on the wall, suggesting that Brad should get on with the painting while Alison got them something to eat – while decorating. He sighed to himself, took off his jacket and set to. If there had been a mirror in the room, he might have been perturbed to see the expression on his face. If Geoff had seen it, he would have put in a requisition for even broader shoulders. Alison did see it later on when she came back but dismissed it. She was getting what she wanted out of life and, for an otherwise intelligent woman, Alison had a great ability to ignore any-thing that didn't quite fit in with what she wanted. She wanted Brad to be happy and so she assumed he was. She could have avoided a lot of heartache with a little more perception, could Alison.

Back at the foster home, a riotous game of Hungry Hippo was proceeding when Charley, having swallowed her pride, knocked at the door and asked for Robert. But he wouldn't come down and Charley spilled her heart out to Lou who couldn't do anything but pat her on the back and hope that things would work out.

Fraser very tentatively sounded Joanne out about the idea of getting in touch with her father who was supposed to be living in America. He had been an American soldier and had left her mother not knowing that she was having a baby. Joanne shook her head emphatically. She didn't want to get let down again, thank you. But Fraser didn't give up easily.

'He must be a nice man,' he insisted, 'or your mother wouldn't have liked him.' She shook her head again.

'Leave it alone, Fraser,' she said politely but firmly and he nodded his head. But Spuggie saw the look in Fraser's eye and smiled inside.

Charley came in and Speedy, who normally had no time at all for girls, quite surprisingly found himself asking her to stay and play Hungry Hippo. She did, to her own surprise, and they all had a good time. Lou caught Nick's eye and smiled to herself. Maybe it would all work out.

None of which was as surprising as what was happening over at the travellers' camp.

Winston had found himself drawn irresistibly back to Sister Tabitha's caravan and had made his way through the woods, creepy as it was. He sat in the grass, trying to pluck up enough courage to knock at the door. And he might have been sitting there still if they hadn't let Clipper, the lurcher, out for a last leg-cocking session. He ran straight across to his new friend, and before Winston could make a move the van door was open again. Seconds later, he was inside drinking a large cup of sweet, hot cocoa and pouring his heart out to Tabitha who made no judgements of any kind but just listened to the sad little boy who looked as if he was carrying the world on his shoulders.

'I just thought,' started Winston. 'If you had a crystal ball and that ... you could help us get in touch with Gill.'

She smiled and shook her head. 'It's just a glass ball, pet.

Ten quid in Woolworths. It doesn't do anything and it can't tell you anything. It's just for taking money off superstitious old ladies.' She grinned. 'Of both sexes.'

He grinned back.

'When people pass away,' Tabitha went on, 'they pass away and they are at peace and don't let anyone tell you any different. If you want to do something for your friend's memory, light a candle.'

'I don't go to church,' said Winston quickly.

She shook her head again. 'Doesn't have to be in a church. Can be anywhere. Just do it and say goodbye. Then you'll feel better.'

And Winston nodded.

He skipped his way home. Tabitha was right. He felt better already.

CHAPTER THREE

Geoff's major concern is always to keep Byker Grove going. He's like the skipper of a very old dearly beloved tramp steamer that chugs along comfortingly most of the time but is inclined just now and again to cause some heart stopping by not quite being in the best of health. Maintenance of the building was supposed to be taken care of by the Council but Geoff has a healthy dislike of things bureaucratic and usually prefers to make his own arrangements with friendly brick-layers and plumbers. That way he gets a good job done and also keeps Byker Grove out of a lot more accounts files, which is a good thing when politicians are looking for ways of saving money. Geoff mused, as he plugged around the outside of the old grey building, that it was a curious thing about saving Council money. It didn't matter how much was 'saved' on paper there was never any trace of it when it came to doing something worthwhile.

Being Geoff, he regularly made his way round the building looking for signs of cracking and general decay. This particular day, the sun was shining and the birds were singing and the signs were pretty good – no major paint flaking, no broken windows, the roof tiles all still intact even after the strong winds of the last few days. As he walked back into the dark hall he did spot something, though. The light from the back window showed that some kind of liquid had been spilled on the shiny floor. He scraped at it with a fingernail. It was wax, not liquid. But it was an odd sort of wax, purple or dark red. He sniffed at it and there was an odd, pungent, even alien smell to it. He sniffed again and frowned just as Alison came in, lips tight, forehead corrugated. He took in her general attitude and sighed inwardly.

'Up before your breakfast, you are, aren't you?' he said, hoping to jolly her along, but she just shot a glance at him and walked past into the kitchen. He followed her, watching as she made tea. Her movements were quick and angry and she clattered the cups together noisily. She saw him watching and grimaced an apology. 'Sorry,' she muttered. 'Couldn't sleep.'

He asked her why but she just gave him a cup of tea and told him it was nothing she couldn't handle and he had to be content with that. He sniffed at his finger again and she looked at him as he held it out to her.

Alison's nose wrinkled. 'Wax?' she said. 'Candle wax?' She sniffed again. 'But it's got a really nasty smell.'

Neither of them could quite place what the smell reminded them of and soon they got on with the rest of the day. Geoff continued with his tour of inspection and Alison started getting the stuff ready for her talk about handicrafts in emerging nations. She was so engrossed in this that the light touch on her arm nearly sent her spinning through the window. She looked round, furious but disarmed almost immediately by the candle power of Paul Skerrett's smile.

'Hi,' he said. 'Sorry. I didn't mean to make you jump.' She had to smile back.

'I'd hate to be around if you did mean to make someone jump,' and they both smiled again. Then there was a little pause and she looked at him questioningly.

'Ah,' he said. 'Sorry. Yes. I was wondering if whatsisname was around.'

She shook her head and denied knowing any whatsisname but they settled for Geoff. Paul had come back to check when would be the best time to talk to the club members and Alison gave him a cup of tea and they spent a pleasant fifteen minutes or so, chatting. Paul was really trying hard to be pleasant and for the first couple of minutes it worked like a Swiss watch. But Alison was just a little bit older than Paul's usual targets and she very quickly saw through him and his very accomplished chatter. Which meant that when Geoff came back with news of more candle wax in odd places, Alison was looking a bit sideways at Paul and he was wondering where he'd gone wrong.

Alison nodded to him curtly and shot off and Geoff took him into the office, wondering why Alison had so obviously taken against what appeared to Geoff to be a fairly normal sort of lad despite the odd ideas and the earring. He listened carefully as Paul led off, talking first about Gill and then about the regrettable increase in joy-riding in the area.

Geoff held up his hand and Paul stopped. 'I'm not trying to be rude,' said Geoff. 'But what has Gill's death got to do with you?'

'Paul nodded. 'Any man's death diminishes me. Never send to seek for whom the bell tolls. It tolls for thee,' he quoted. 'Or words to that effect.'

Geoff leaned back in his chair. That was all he needed, a Jehovah's Witness running round the place. But Paul just pulled out another disarming smile and told Geoff that the idea would be for the kids of the Grove to go on the Great North Run carrying banners that said 'CARS KILL PEOPLE', together with a huge photograph of Gill. Geoff said he'd think about it and Paul sprang off down the drive like a modern version of Springheeled Jack. Alison and Geoff watched him go.

Alison voiced her suspicion first. 'I have,' she volunteered, 'a very funny feeling about that lad.'

Geoff turned and looked at her. There was just the hint of a twinkle in his eye. 'Aye,' he replied. 'Aye. There's nothing like spending half an hour in the company of a genuine fanatic, is there? For persuading you just how nice it is to be sane.' They both looked back at Paul's disappearing figure and fell silent again. It was all very well to make jokes but each time you got a chance to peep behind the smiling eyes and the charming grin, there was the undeniable feeling that there was something else going on inside, nothing that you could put your finger on.

Alison shook her head, impatient with herself, Paul wasn't her problem. But Geoff was still staring after him down the road. Paul Skerrett was trouble. That much Geoff knew. He didn't know how much but he did know he wanted it kept well away from Byker Grove. He turned back to Alison and voiced the question that was bothering him most of all.

'Nicola Dobson,' he asked. 'Is she serious about this lad or what?'

Alison shrugged. What was serious, what was not, she didn't know and she didn't particularly feel like finding out.

Geoff listened to her grizzle for a moment and then quite firmly and quietly told her what her job at the Grove was and that part of it was doing what he, the leader, asked her to and, in this case, he wanted her to find out how serious things were between a lad neither of them liked and one of the kids they were both supposed to be looking out for. She stood, white-faced, for a second and then nodded.

'Sorry, man, Geoff,' she faltered. 'Sorry. I have things on my mind.'

He nodded. He very rarely used the big stick but this seemed to be the right time. Then he put his arm round Alison's shoulders and told her that she was also entitled to his time if she had anything she wanted to talk to him about. She gave him a watery smile.

'I hope it doesn't come to that,' she said. 'I hope it'll all work out OK.'

And Geoff had to be content with that, although he hoped and prayed that things would turn out all right for Alison and Brad. But Nicola was his prime concern. He looked at his fingernail. Nicola and candle wax.

His mind might have been set at ease if he could have been

with Winston and Kelly as they sat on the wall outside the school waiting for the bus. Winston had unwrapped a huge ceremonial candle and was showing it to Kelly, who privately thought it was way over the top. Also, she didn't know what it was for.

Winston patiently explained again. 'It's just a symbol,' he said. 'It doesn't have to be in a church. It doesn't have to be anywhere special. I just light this and it's like a – ' He stopped, lost for words.

'A tribute?' Kelly said and he nodded gratefully. That was exactly what it was, a tribute to Gill. And he smiled with relief. It had been good talking to Mrs Finney. She just listened and didn't tell you what you ought to be doing and thinking. Kelly interrupted his thoughts.

'So,' said Kelly and her eyes glinted impishly behind her huge glasses. 'Did she tell you your fortune?'

He nodded dourly.

'Aye,' he said heavily. 'She did. And I'm afraid it's bad news for you.' His voice was so solemn that a cold hand clutched at Kelly's heart.

'What?' she demanded. 'What?'

But Winston grinned as he looked away, hiding his face. 'She told us to beware of small women with big glasses.'

And Kelly flicked his ear and he howled with pain and they rolled around and tussled till the bus came and, in fact, of all the people who went to Byker Grove, these two were coping with life better than anyone.

Charley wasn't coping at all – she was sliding deeper and deeper into the pits of depression. Robert was totally unavailable these days, refusing to see her, refusing to speak to her, and spending every hour he could in the gym, torturing himself on the shiny steel machines, determined to prove everybody wrong when they said he wouldn't play football again. Charley rowed with her mother and her father and her brother. In fact, everybody she spoke to, she rowed with, and she banged out of the house that day, deliberately smashing the door shut behind her, almost hoping that she'd broken the glass panel. There, on the doorstep, was a red rose, just one, in a cellophane wrapper. She picked it up, unbelievingly, and saw her name written in a strange hand on the outside. She looked quickly up and down the road, feeling as if somebody must be watching her and giggling. It wasn't a pleasant feeling and she stalked off quickly, stuffing the flower into her duffle bag as she went.

When she got to the Grove, full because it was a grey, cold day, she looked for Nicola or Donna, someone her own age to talk to. She found them all right but they were in full flight, talking about Donna's current obsession. This was that Nicola was getting much too involved with Paul and didn't know anything about him, not where he lived, nothing. Where had he suddenly sprung from, Donna wanted to know. But Nicola just looked at her with that understanding, forgiving smile which said that Donna was just jealous and which made Donna want to kick her shins.

'It makes no difference,' said Nicola serenely and smiled again. 'I don't care where he lives or what he does or where he came from.'

Donna looked round at Charley and rolled her eyes. Charley grinned and sat down beside them. 'It will make a lot of difference,' Donna persisted, 'if you're trying to find him, after.' Nicola knew what she meant and so did Charley.

'After what?' asked Nicola with a great show of innocence, and Donna flicked her eyebrows up and down to show exactly what she meant, and Nicola told her she was disgusting.

'If I'm disgusting, so are you,' retorted Donna, 'because you knew what I was talking about without asking.' And they all giggled at that.

Nicola put their collective minds at rest. 'There's nothing going on, Donna. Nothing,' she sighed. Which wasn't entirely true. Things *were* going on but nothing that Nicola was going to tell Donna about. Some things were private and if you told Donna Bell anything, it was a bit like going on *Wogan* with nothing on because you'd never be able to hide again. Donna was the equivalent of the old-fashioned town crier except that she was a bit inclined to add little bits of her own to any news she happened to pick up; little tasty additions which made things just that bit more interesting.

She turned to Charley to see if she could stir anything up there. Robert hadn't been much in evidence recently and Donna thought he'd probably got over the glamour bit now that Marilyn Charlton was just a person again and not a pop star. 'You and Robert split up, have you?' Nicola was appalled to hear her ask. Charley went very quiet. When she did speak, her voice was a bit unsteady. She also tried a little smile which didn't fool Miss Bell for a minute.

'I think he's embarrassed,' said Charley. 'He thought he was going to be running round as soon as he got out of the wheelchair and it's not worked out that way, so far.' She smiled again to indicate that the discussion was over but Donna went in for the kill, just for practice really, like a cat playing with a mouse before biting its head off.

'It really hasn't been your year, has it, Marilyn, pet?' she said sweetly. 'First of all you fall in love with a cripple, then you make a mess of your record and now even Ironside doesn't want to have anything to do with you. I should change me scent or something, if I was you.'

Nicola knew Donna had a low opinion of herself, mainly caused by her mother leaving and her dad getting wed again, and she knew her friend would strike in all directions at once if she felt the urge, just because. But this was queen-size bitchery even for Donna, who was now grinning and waiting for tears. Nicola was just about to say something but this had been a hard year for Charley and she had grown tougher. Donna's mindless little nastiness hardly compared with her real troubles.

'Thanks, Donna, for reminding me,' replied Charley, just as saccharin sweet as Donna had been. 'It's always nice to have a friend to jog your memory.'

And she walked off to get herself a cup of tea, leaving Donna wounded on the field of battle and feeling just a little foolish. She opened her mouth to add a bit more acid but Nicola caught her eye and shook her head.

'Leave it, I should,' said Nicola. 'The last shot was hers. Anything you say now's going to sound stupid.'

Donna grimaced and let Charley go. What she had done, though, was put a little bit of steel back into Charley's spine and while she drank the tea, she made a plan. A plan which took her out of the Grove and on to a bus and right down to the gym where Robert was still pumping iron.

She went straight in and waited till he was finished and out of the shower with the beads of water still in his curly brown hair. She longed to stretch out her hand to brush them away but she held herself taut and firm.

'We have to talk, Robert,' she said, as she walked along beside him. He wanted to evade it but she wouldn't let him. She had too much love invested in this tall, shy boy to let it go without a struggle. He said he had nothing to offer her but she fought back. She told him *she* had things to offer *him*, that it wasn't just one-sided; she was a person too, with needs and wants. She talked to him and showed how much he meant to her until he fell silent and looked at her with new eyes.

'All right,' he conceded at last. 'But not now. Not here.' And he gave her the first real smile she'd seen on his face for many a long week. 'Tell you the truth, Charley,' he admitted. 'I'm knackered and I really feel I have to be at full strength to cope with you.'

She stepped back and studied him carefully and then,

taking full advantage of the fact that he was knackered whatever that meant, leaned the full length of her young body against him, pressed him against the wall and kissed him until he squeaked. Then she let him go, both of them breathless, and said she expected to hear from him soon or he could expect more of the same. Then she went out and Robert glared at his coach who was pulling faces and making suggestive movements through the window of his office. Robert wasn't all that displeased, though, as he made his slow way home.

Paul, in the meantime, was also making a few plans. Oddly enough, for someone who inspired so much hero-worship in Nicola, and instant distrust in older people, Paul was fairly straightforward. He knew what he wanted and he knew how he wanted the world to be. He had been brought up in a vicarage and until he was about twelve had trusted in God to keep the world right for people to live in. But, increasingly, as he saw atrocities reported on television and in the newspapers, and as his father evaded his questions about the way man was ruining the planet, he came to the conclusion that either there was no God or else he was very inefficient. There was a third alternative, of course, that God knew what was going on and didn't care much about stopping it but Paul couldn't have stayed with his father if he'd accepted that.

Being a single-minded youth, he set out to save the world on his own. There wouldn't be much he could do but he had to make a start somewhere. So he joined a slightly mysterious outfit that called itself the Green Brigade and that was dedicated firstly to stopping people driving big cars, and secondly to stopping them driving any cars at all. He didn't follow through on what would replace cars. That wasn't Paul's problem.

The Green Brigade on the Tyne wasn't big. In fact it was

Paul and a voice on the other end of a telephone and various lieutenants recruited by Paul from time to time to help with one-off projects. Being Paul, these were often young girls. And this was what Paul had in mind for Nicola. Except that every time he looked at Nicola, he thought less about cars and more about other things. He liked being with Nicola very much indeed.

The feeling was mutual and Nicola ran to meet him. She had been five minutes early but the time for holding back and being cool was long gone. She gave him a big squeeze and a quick kiss to keep him warm for later. Then, stepping back and looking at him, she laughed out loud. He grinned back at her.

'What?' said Paul but she just shrugged and smiled at him.

'I like being with you,' said Nicola simply and blushed but didn't mind. She *did* like him and she didn't care who knew it. She was free, pink and sixteen and she could do what she liked. Actually she was free, pink and nearly sixteen but for what Nicola had in mind, sixteen was better. Paul talked to her as they went along and she noticed that they were heading for the posh end of town.

'What are we actually doing, anyway?' she wanted to know and he told her freely and frankly. They were looking for big, expensive, planet-ruining cars and the best place to find them was in the richer areas of town, which went without saying. Paul was quite blatant and obvious about it, using a notebook and noting down address after address. He told Nicola the thing that would get them noticed was being furtive. If you saw someone watching you, he went on, you should go right up to that person and ask them something, always smiling, always pleasant, and always looking them right in the eye.

'Why are we noting down where all these big cars are, though?' she worried and he told her that too. That was the point of the date on Saturday morning at the crack of dawn.

People with big cars were going to find themselves severely inconvenienced.

Paul was fascinating to Nicola's young mind. He said things that made sense. He looked deep into her eyes and told her about places where the air was clear and the animals could live their lives without interference from man, where the sea was crystal clear right down to the white sand at the bottom, where there was no carbon monoxide, no petrol fumes, no filth, no grime, no birds choking to death in oil, no rainforests massacred to make plywood for Japanese building projects. She listened and was captivated all over again. If Paul had asked her anything at that moment, she would have done it. Anything at all in the whole wide world. She looked over Paul's shoulder and saw a young policeman watching them with obvious suspicion. Their clothes, bright and cheap and casual, made it clear that they didn't belong in this district. The people who lived round here only had grown-up children or children who wore blazers and proper leather shoes. The young policeman spoke a word or two into his radio and made towards the pair. Paul was quicker, though, and was already halfway across the road, sporting his best middle-class accent and showing the officer an address.

'Hello, officer,' said Paul and smiled deep into the officer's face. He had no option, really, except to smile back, even though Paul and Nicola looked like spies for a strange tribe of exotic natives from over the hill. He looked at the address Paul was asking him about and gave them detailed instructions about how to get there. Paul grabbed Nicola's hand and they hurried off, turning to wave their thanks.

'How do you do that?' asked Nicola admiringly. 'I die every time they look at me. Even if I've done nothing.' And Paul explained once more. The secret is not to look furtive, always look straight at people.

What they didn't know was that our young copper had just

56

been on a course and one of the lessons he had learned was that you can't always tell what somebody is like just by looking at them. He had also been told about the man who comes up to you, smiling and looking you in the eye; and then kicks you in the teeth. Unfortunately for Paul and Nicola in the long run, this young policeman remembered their faces and what they were doing.

The address they were making for happened to be the same magic shop where the owner had frightened P.J. and the lads away. Nicola stood and looked at it and felt a ripple of distaste. It really did look like a mouth. You could almost imagine it licking its lips She supposed it was the red of the lights but it was also the demeanour of the place, like a servant who rubbed his hands ever so humbly, but you'd never be able to have a bath without stuffing up the bathroom keyhole.

Paul looked back and waved her on. He was impatient and he also didn't want the copper wondering any more about why they were there. Nicola slowly followed Paul into the shop which was even more unsavoury inside. And her misgivings deepened when the shopkeeper came out actually rubbing his hands and looking her over. She moved herself and her thin blouse out of the light from the doorway and was glad to be wearing jeans. She looked at Paul. She was very surprised to be brought here and even more surprised to hear Paul talking to the man, Tyrone, as if he was an old friend.

All the while Tyrone and Paul talked, Tyrone's eyes were flickering across at Nicola. She paid no attention, hoping that she and Paul would soon be gone. Then something she heard made her listen carefully. Paul's voice was lower but Nicola's hearing was acute.

'Saturday morning,' she heard him murmur.

'Both of you?' asked Tyrone. 'Her?'

And they both turned and looked at Nicola, Paul with a reassuring grin, the older man with a look of frank doubt which was not much better than the leer he had used before. Paul held his hand out for Nicola to join them.

'Come on over here and meet Tyrone,' he ordered, just a little peevishly when she didn't move fast enough. She nodded and Tyrone shook her hand.

'Any friend of Paul's,' he said, smiling, and it was odd because the creepy manner had gone, almost as if it had just been deliberate, to see how it affected her. Nicola liked him even less. Bad enough to be an old lecher; even worse to do it on purpose, just for effect. But the Tyrone she was talking to now seemed as normal as anyone she had ever met, almost affable.

She listened while he and Paul discussed what it was that Paul had come to the shop for and they could have been talking science fiction for all she understood. Silicon bases, tactile strength and stickability all featured heavily. Then they were finished and Paul took a couple of bottles from the shopkeeper, gave one to her and they were about to leave when Tyrone called them back. He hesitated, then nodded towards Nicola.

'Your young friend,' he asked Paul. 'How committed is she? To our ideals?'

Paul shrugged and looked at Nicola. 'There she is,' he answered. 'Ask her yourself!'

Tyrone looked at her and Nicola told him that she was committed to Paul's ideal of rescuing the world we live in for future generations. Tyrone looked impressed and said that maybe they could do some more business some time, at which Paul looked just a shade wary. Tyrone grinned at him and said there was nothing to worry about. It was just a delivery job and he'd see how things went on Saturday morning before committing anybody any further.

Then they were out of the shop and walking away, Nicola feeling breathless and sweating, as if she had just run a mile. She still did not know what was going to happen on Saturday morning and told Paul so, but he just bathed her in his biggest and best smile and said it was going to be a great surprise for little Miss Dobson. She got cross and said she wasn't all that little and he said he knew that. And they put their arms round each other and went on from there. What they did, doesn't concern us, only them, but it was the best way either of them knew of spending free time together.

Back at the shop, Tyrone had a long telephone conversation with a friend of his, the gist of which was that Paul had a new friend and they would all be in business again very soon. He put the phone down and went into the back room and started making a little surprise which Paul and Nicola heard about quite a bit later.

Geoff was getting obsessed with red wax. It seemed that there were traces of it everywhere, even in the most unlikely places, on windowsills, on the stairs leading up to the roof, everywhere. He stopped Fraser and asked him if he knew anything about it. Fraser didn't but he also thought Geoff was making a mountain out of a molehill. 'It'll be someone playing silly beggars, Geoff, man,' he said, puzzled. 'Treasure-hunting or something.' Geoff searched his face doubtfully. 'They'll be doing it, whoever they are, then following you round and laughing theirselves sick watching you finding it. You know this lot, Geoff. They can make mischief out of anything.'

Geoff was only partly reassured but Fraser's argument gained credence when P.J., Speedy and Duncan surged past, chased loudly, with much giggling and banter, by Jemma, Debbie and Joanne. Geoff called after them but they either didn't hear, or didn't want to, and just bubbled on and up the stairs. Geoff started after them but Fraser caught his arm. 'Hey,' said Fraser. 'I'll do it. I'll find out what's going on.' Geoff nodded. He was right. Fraser slipped upstairs at a fast trot and Geoff went into his office to see how much money they didn't have left for the rest of the financial year.

Upstairs, Fraser found the schemers just by tracing the noise. They were in full conference mode when he went in. He asked them if they knew anything about red wax and they just looked at each other and shrugged. They didn't and Fraser believed them. 'What are you doing, then?' he asked and they looked at each other again, doubtfully. They weren't sure whether to tell Fraser, him not being on the management committee, but he soon persuaded them by threatening to tickle Debbie. He had hit on the committee's one weakness – Debbie will say anything to avoid being tickled. So they unfolded the plan which was actually a pretty good one. They were going to hold an acid house party, sell tickets and raise enough money for a memorial to Gill. They didn't know what kind of memorial but they reckoned they could sort that out as and when. It was more important to rake in the cash first.

'Good idea,' Fraser nodded approvingly. 'Whose house are you having it at?'

There was a little silence as the committee looked at one another and Fraser shook his head wearily. Were they actually planning to hold an illegal acid house rave-up in the Grove? P.J. explained that there wasn't going to be any real acid because none of them could get any. Speedy started to say that none of them knew what it was either, but P.J. thought that was uncool and shut him up. Then they set about persuading Fraser what a really great idea it was.

'What about gatecrashers?' asked Fraser practically and this set them thinking. They'd all heard of parties which had turned into riots because of gatecrashers. 'It's not a good idea,' persisted Fraser. 'Where would you have it, anyway?'

They had thought of doing it down in the cellar but Fraser threw cold water on that too. The cellar was not only off limits since Spuggie and her chess-playing convict friend had been caught down there, it was also locked. They all grinned and Duncan triumphantly produced his picklocks which he reckoned could open anything. Fraser wavered a little but then wanted to know about music. Nobody he knew had enough records. Debbie had the answer to that one.

'P.J.'s got thousands of records,' she piped up. Jemma looked at her in disbelief and Speedy was astounded.

'P.J. keeps all them records under his bed,' he exclaimed. 'How do you know about them?' Debbie just grinned and linked arms with P.J. and Jemma grew hot and cold. She was getting left behind! Debbie had only just latched on to P.J. and already she'd been in his bedroom! As a matter of fact, she hadn't, but Debbie wasn't going to say, having noticed the gratifying effect her remark was having on all present. Duncan was grinning like a Cheshire Cat, Speedy's jaw had hit the floor and Jemma had turned green. Duncan stopped grinning, though, when Jemma slid her arm through his and announced that she'd been in plenty of lads' bedrooms.

One of Fraser's great strengths is that he has an open mind. He listened to the general chatter and thought that there might just be the germ of a good idea buried in there somewhere. If they kept the tickets reasonable, had a couple of reliable bouncers and kept Denton Burn out, it might just turn out to be a good night. He nodded while they looked at him. They didn't need his approval but they respected his opinion. 'Let's have a look in this cellar,' he said and they trooped out, with Duncan fingering his picklocks like the jailer in a Clint Eastwood movie. Jemma and Debbie followed, sniggering, and Duncan had the uneasy feeling that he'd been picked out for something. It wasn't too hard for him to figure out that he was going to be Jemma's date for the party. The worst of it was, he wasn't sure he actually minded. She had a sort of way with her that made her a lot of fun to be with.

Winston, on the other hand, was regretting what looked like the end of a friendship. His visits to the grave had finally caused Kelly to snap. The problem was that, although he was really getting over Gill, he couldn't just call a halt to it all at once. Kelly was a great one for drawing lines under things and saying, right, ended. Winston, like most lads, came and went and Kelly couldn't cope with that. So he sat and tidied the stones obsessively in the chill wind, until he looked up to find a shadow falling over him as he took out Gill's photograph and stood it up on the little mound. It fell over and he picked it up and stood and faced the man who had come up behind him.

'Is that him?' the man asked and reached over to take the photograph. He looked at the young, wilful face that was already locked into eternity with no clue at all as to the kind of man he might have been. He took Winston's hand and led him to a nearby seat and for the second time in a couple of days Winston found himself talking to a grown-up who seemed to know how he felt.

This man was a vicar of some kind and he listened patiently to the young lad's tale. Winston looked him straight in the eye and told him that he didn't believe in God but Mr Skerrett (the vicar and Paul Skerrett's father) laughed and said that didn't matter. Winston didn't have to believe in God, that was his privilege. Luckily, though, God believed in Winston. The lad thought about it and started to shake his head until he realised that there was something quite comforting in what Mr Skerrett had said. Now he felt he could ask what was really troubling him. Winston fell silent for a brief moment and then he fixed Mr Skerrett with his clear blue eyes and Skerrett sighed when he saw what was coming, for he had no real answer to give.

'When you die,' Winston started, and then stopped. 'When you die, where does your soul go? Where do *you* go?'

Mr Skerrett took his time about replying and after a little

while he realised that Winston was no longer listening. He stood up. 'Come and see me,' said Skerrett. 'Maybe we can work something out.'

But Winston didn't think he ever would.

Back at the Grove, the dance committee looked at the cellar. It wouldn't really be suitable – it was dusty and filthy and full of machinery. So they started back up the stairs. Then they heard a noise. It would be Geoff for a pound and they were in deep trouble. The noise stopped. 'Somebody'll have to go and see if the coast's clear,' whispered P.J. Debbie volunteered. They eased the door open and she slipped out and peeped round the corner. Nothing. So she slid along to the next corner and looked round that one too. There was a slight figure in a black jacket leaning in the shadows, one of the Byker Grovers, obviously, half familiar but she couldn't put a name to him. She was about to hiss at him to see if Geoff was about when his head turned slowly and she could make out his features a bit more clearly. Her blood ran cold and she scuttled back to the others as fast as she could go.

They didn't bother her with questions, they could see how badly frightened she was, even by Debbie's standards. Fraser talked to her quietly and managed to persuade her that she couldn't have seen what she said she saw. The others took her back to the general room, all talking very loud and overly cheerful, while Fraser went back to the corridor. There didn't seem to be anything there until he bent down and looked at the floor where there were unmistakable traces of red wax. He felt one with his finger and stood up with his face long and serious. The wax was still soft and faintly warm to the touch. He went to find Geoff and Geoff went back to the spot with him. They both stood looking at the wax. And Geoff looked at Fraser.

'Who was it she said she saw?' demanded Geoff and Fraser

told him and Geoff looked down at the wax again and this time his face was troubled.

'Nothing about this to anyone!' Geoff declared, and Fraser shook his head.

The stable door was already wide open, of course, and the rumour factory that was Byker Grove hummed with the story of what Debbie Dobson had seen in the dark, spooky corridor at the top of the cellar steps.

She lay at home in bed that night. Her mum and dad had made sure that she and Jemma shared a room since the last lot of nightmares and Debbie was truly grateful for her rotten little sister that night. Jemma was full of it and made Debbie tell her the whole story all over again, because it was Gill that Debbie had seen, or Gill's ghost, and Jemma wanted to hear every detail. Had there been, for instance, any blood on him and were his features all smashed up and rotting? Things like that. Debbie pulled a face but in fact Jemma was making the apparition less frightening by forcing Debbie to talk about it and face it. They talked most of the night and they were still awake when Nicola slipped out at half-past four the next morning to meet Paul. They wondered if she was eloping but Jemma slipped into the bathroom and found her toothbrush. So it definitely wasn't that.

No, it wasn't. Nicola was helping to stick large and very-hard-to-shift pieces of card to the windscreens of big, expensive cars, and she and Paul giggled while they did it. It would take hours to scrape them clean, he explained, and maybe it would make people think twice before polluting the atmosphere with filthy petrol fumes.

It made one person think twice. This was a doctor who got a six o'clock emergency call to go to a young baby who was in dire distress, fighting for breath. He thought several times as he desperately scraped at the card which would not come off, before running back into the house to call a taxi. Not all cars are killers, as the card said. Some are life-savers.

Luckily the taxi came in time. But what had been an ecological prank could have turned into a tragedy, although Paul – in the blind sureness of youth – didn't take account of things like that.

CHAPTER FOUR

The news of Debbie's ghostly experience spread like wildfire and Geoff could see he was going to have a major problem keeping a lid on it. It was bad enough kids thinking ghostly thoughts and seeing apparitions all over the place but next thing the local newspapers would get hold of it and then things would really get out of hand. He pondered long and hard and even got Debbie in to talk about it. He knew very well how suggestible she was, witness all the problems they had had when the lads had terrified the life out of her, making her watch that video.

Geoff's a kind man and he talked slowly and patiently to little Deborah with the big brown eyes and the mind full of horrors.

'I know there's no such thing as ghosts,' she insisted. 'But I did see something, Geoff, and it was something weird and it had a leather jacket and nobody round here's ever worn a leather jacket except Gill.' And she looked deep into Geoff's eyes and tried very hard to make him understand that she really had seen something and she didn't know what it was and she hoped more than anyone else that there was a reasonable explanation for it.

Geoff patted her on the head and sent her off and worried twice as much. It wasn't Gill, that much he knew. But he did have a prowler dropping red wax and that might be even worse than a friendly spirit. There was a knock at the door and Kelly and Winston stood there, Kelly looking solemn and important, Winston just looking put out and angry.

'What's up with you two?' Geoff demanded and Kelly shoved Winston, who shoved her back.

'Winston's got something to show you,' said Kelly quickly and Winston glared at her and produced a big bag. 'Show him!' hissed Kelly, and Winston gave her another angry look, then opened the bag and put a big red candle on Geoff's desk. He picked it up and looked at it.

'It's not me,' stated the little lad angrily. 'That's never been lit.'

It was true. Geoff turned the candle round in his hands and looked at Winston. He asked him where he'd got it and why, and Winston shook his head stubbornly. Tabitha had thought about the wisdom of giving a young boy such an object with all its possible connections with witchcraft and fortune-telling and ouija boards and such-like, and she had remembered the bad reputation travelling people had anyway in most places. So she'd given Winston the candle, hoping it would help him say goodbye to his dead friend. She had also asked him not to tell anyone where he'd got it, and he had kept his word. He just shook his head stubbornly at Geoff. 'I can't tell you, man, Geoff,' he protested. 'I promised. I can't!' And Geoff had to be content with that. At least it wasn't Winston.

Meanwhile the pack of lads were also thinking about the figure Debbie had seen. These were hard-headed lads, not given much to fancy thoughts. They were often able to frighten each other with tales of ghosties and ghoulies and things that go bump in the night but in the broad light of day they had a much more prosaic view of what might be hanging round the corridors of Byker Grove.

'It'll be another of these dam alkies,' P.J. pronounced.

They nodded. From time to time, vagrants and winos would sneak in the Grove after lights out, making a right stink until they were moved on by Geoff.

Speedy agreed. 'It's about time something was done. There are even more winos about now. You can't walk anywhere these days without them shouting and swearing at you.' He shook his head. 'I don't see, me, how anyone can get hooked on that stuff. I mean, have you ever tasted it? I'd have to be right hard up to get that stuff down me neck.'

He stopped, to find that the room had gone very quiet, and cursed himself when he saw the way Fraser was looking at him, two bright spots of red high on his cheekbones. Everybody was thinking the same thing. Fraser's mam was in a unit drying out from drinking too much wine and not eating enough. Speedy started to say how sorry he was but Fraser just shook his head. His mother wasn't that kind of alky. His mother had just been sick, that's all, and she was getting better.

'What we have got to think about,' said Fraser into the silence, 'is what we are going to do if there *is* someone hanging about. There's no way we can have any kind of disco with a tramp in the Grove frightening all the little lasses.

They agreed and decided that they would have to smoke him out, however difficult it was. Debbie still wasn't convinced, though. She was fairly certain it hadn't been a tramp. There had been something 'other' about the figure she had seen, although she couldn't say exactly what. So they just assumed it was another one of Debbie's fantasies and agreed to follow their first plan. Find out who it was and shift them. Simple.

It was still Saturday morning. Brad rolled over lazily, glad of the lie-in. Glad, that is, until the telephone rang and the sweet appealing voice of Alison, the voice he would once have died for, ruined his day by reminding him that they had a date with some paint and some wallpaper and a little terraced house. He groaned as he put the telephone down. They wouldn't even be on their own. Spuggie and Joanne had offered to help, and their bright sparrow-like enquiring eyes would be all over the place. The whole morning would be filled with nudging and giggling and snorting. The flap of the letterbox went and he went down, bleary-eyed, to pick up the post.

Ten minutes later, he was sitting at the table, trembling, a cup of coffee in his hand and an awe-inspiring prospect opening out in front of him. He hadn't ever really thought anything would come of it but a couple of months previously Brad had replied to an advert looking for a photographer to go to the Antarctic with a research vessel for a year. He'd had an interview and then another and then got a thanks but no thanks, although they'd been kind enough to say he'd come second. The letter in front of him said that the man who'd come first had contracted hepatitis, and if Brad was still available at short notice to take his place they'd appreciate a reverse charge telephone call.

He went back upstairs, knowing there was no way he could go away and leave Alison. Even while he shaved and changed and packed his bag, he still thought there was no way he would go. When he was getting in his car, he realised he was talking out loud and had been the whole time he'd been getting ready. When he recognised what he was saying to himself, he knew there was no way he could stay and paint houses. He was reciting his father's old Turkish proverb.

'When the house is built, the man dies.' Over and over.

'When the house is built, the man dies.'

And he was still saying it to himself as he stood at Geoff's desk and wrote a short note. He said it once more in the little terraced house not even knowing he was being unbelievably cruel as he painted a goodbye to Alison on the wall of their future home. The proverb echoed in his head all the way down the motorway. It may be echoing in his head still. It may echo there for ever.

It was the merest twist of fate that Alison was late getting to the house. Normally she was the earliest of early birds, especially when she was going to be doing something she loved. So she had been on time at the Gallaghers' to pick up Joanne and Spuggie, today's amateur labouring force. They had been a little late because Joanne was in the middle of a

69

question and answer session with Fraser which she hadn't really seen the point of. Spuggie had realised, halfway through, what Fraser was getting at and had sat, not daring to breathe, as Fraser asked seemingly innocent questions about Joanne's early days, about her birthday and exactly where she'd been born. He had listened with a half-interested air which stopped her realising that she was being expertly pumped and that Fraser was going to use these facts to set in motion a train of events that would eventually find her GI father. She finally did get fed up, though, and shot out to the car with Spuggie.

'Hi ho, hi ho, it's off to work we go,' the three of them carolled in the car on the way to the Gingerbread Cottage, as Spuggie had christened it. Spuggie had also secretly marked it out as a very cool place to live if ever it became surplus to Alison and Brad's needs.

They took a short cut Alison knew well, one which took her past a shop where she could get a couple of pairs of disposable gloves, small size, Joanne and Spuggie for the use of. When she went in the shop, Spuggie and Joanne peered about the way little girls do, missing nothing. It was a bright and cheerful morning and who knew what they might see.

What they did see was quite surprising. Spuggie tugged Joanne's arm. 'Hey up!' she muttered. 'Look!'

Joanne looked and saw Nicola Dobson and the creep from the Green Brigade hurtle round the corner and throw a sort of newspaper bag over a nearby hedge. Then they slowed right down and put their arms round each other to saunter along – butter wouldn't melt. Joanne's eyebrows rose almost up to her hairline as a police car zipped round the corner and stopped alongside the pair. The young policewoman inside slowly got out of the car and went across to Paul and Nicola with that special slow walk that young coppers always use when they want to appear in complete command of the situation. It was unlucky for her that Alison came out of the shop just at that moment and saw what was going on.

Alison has a healthy interest in civil rights and this sometimes means that she will take anybody's side against the police. This applies double when the victim is someone she knows is incapable of doing anything wrong; Nicola, that is. Paul, on this occasion, was innocent by association. The policewoman, who had no grounds for suspicion other than the fact that Paul and Nicola were young and laughing, thought she had jumped into a food mixer when Alison demanded to know what was going on. She just pointed out that some cars had been vandalised.

'And you're stopping all the young people you pass, are you?' demanded Alison. 'To make sure?' The policewoman looked from one to the other. She could see she was on a hiding to nothing here and was pretty pleased to get a squawk on the radio to attend a traffic incident. She looked at them all very hard to make sure they knew they were getting off lightly, got into the car and drove off, hoping her ears hadn't gone red.

Alison looked at the young couple. 'What was all that about?' she asked. Paul just shrugged but Alison was intrigued and a little puzzled when Nicola looked to one side, unable to meet her gaze properly. 'Can I give you a lift anywhere?' she asked and was again slightly bothered by Nicola who shook her head, even as Paul was thanking her effusively and climbing into the back of the car with Spuggie and Joanne who were in fits of giggles about something. After looking at her watch Alison decided she could leave finding out why they were laughing till later. Brad would be as mad as hell anyway. He always liked Alison to be on time. She dropped the other pair some way down the street and watched the flushed faces of the two little girls in the driving mirror as they pushed each other and sniggered.

She finally stopped worrying about the giggling when

Spuggie and Joanne came back out of the house while she was still bent over unloading the car. She looked at their white faces and half-open mouths and ran past them into the house, certain she was going to find Brad injured or dead. It might have been better if she had, for when she saw the short, cruel message on the wall something died inside Alison. She felt her mouth part in a stupid half-grin. It had to be a joke. Brad had to be hiding somewhere, teaching her a lesson for being late. Then she read the words again. 'Sorry! It would never have worked. Love Brad.' She heard the two little girls come and stand quietly beside her.

'Well,' she said brightly, turning to them. 'At least we don't have to bother doing any painting, do we?'

When they got to the Grove, she shooed them off and went to look for Geoff. His face told her the same story. He was sitting at the desk reading Brad's note. She held out a hand for it, read it and gave it back to him. The half-smile on her face had grown more than a little bitter in the time it had taken to get to the Grove. She tried to make a joke out of it but Geoff wasn't fooled for long. She shook her head and he could see the sparkle of unshed tears in her eyes. He put his arms round her and held her lightly and felt the deep inner tremble as she fought not to cry, not to give herself away. Soon she stepped back and tried a little smile. It was a good try, in the circumstances, and Geoff mentally gave her A for effort. She needed the day off and Geoff knew that better than she did. So she went home and Geoff ripped up Brad's note, wishing it was his neck.

Fraser knocked on the door. Spuggie had told him that Brad had scarpered and Geoff started to say that he appreciated Fraser popping by but that Alison had already gone. Fraser was nonplussed. He hadn't come in to offer sympathy, he was after Brad's job. Geoff was taken aback at his cheek but Fraser was stoutly determined and got straight to the point.

'I've got to get a flat and get me mam back out the rehab,' he stated baldly. 'I canna afford to be sentimental about Alison and Brad.'

Geoff said he'd think about it but Fraser stood his ground and said he wanted more than that. Geoff thought about it and the more he thought about it, the more he reckoned it was a good idea.

'Park your behind,' ordered Geoff. Then he picked up the telephone, while Fraser sat and grinned delightedly as Geoff fought the good fight on his behalf.

In Head Office, they were never any match for the portly custodian of the Grove, and for every reason they put forward for not employing the lad, Geoff had a good reason why they should. Finally he put the phone down with a grin and gave Fraser the thumbs up.

'Thanks, man, Geoff,' said Fraser gruffly. Not many people had gone to bat for Fraser in the past and what Geoff had done meant a lot to him. He cleared his throat again and stood up, anxious to get out of the office before he did anything uncool, like bursting out sobbing which would have been very high on the uncool scale.

Geoff looked a bit surprised. Didn't Fraser want to know how much he would get a week? Fraser shook his head. 'I know I won't get cheated if it has anything to do with you.' And it was Geoff's turn to clear his throat.

Then Fraser did go out and ran straight into a reception committee which had been convened by Spuggie and consisted of the Dobson duo, herself and Joanne. 'How much money will you be getting?' Spuggie demanded. Fraser shook his head. 'When you do know, will you tell us?' she persisted. He shook his head again and looked at his sister.

'What do you want to know for, anyway. It'll all be going in the bank,' he said. And it would, because this was going to be his mother's coming-home fund. Spuggie looked a little downcast. She had heard about the mega gob-smacking disco party they were planning to have, and the nearest thing she had to party gear was getting so short, it was nearly indecent. She'd been hoping that Fraser might be able to lend her a bit to get something new. She couldn't very well ask, though, if it was going to help get her mother out of hospital.

Joanne saw the expression and guessed the reason behind it so she told Fraser what was on Spuggie's mind. Which set him off on a rapid rethinking process. It was all very well helping to arrange an illicit out-of-hours bash when you were just a club member, a mere foot soldier. But, with a sinking feeling, he realised he now had a foot in the management camp. He was probably as high as a corporal and anything out of the legal norm would have to be reported to Geoff.

'You can't go to that,' he informed Spuggie, who blew him a raspberry and told him he couldn't stop her. 'You're not old enough,' he said.

And then Jemma stuck her oar in, having been quiet for much longer than usual. 'Old enough for what?' she asked. 'What's going on? Can I go? Where are you going? I'm twelve. Is that old enough?'

Debbie tugged at her arm, wanting to know where P.J. had gone, and Jemma shrugged her off grumpily. Debbie was really pathetic these days, following P.J. round like the tail on a kite. It didn't help either when she kept grinning annoyingly – Jemma was starting to feel more than a little left out. Debbie was also very unforthcoming when Jemma asked questions such as had P.J. tried anything on yet and what would Debbie do when he did, if he did? These were essential items of information and there was nobody else Jemma could ask.

'Why do you want to know where he is, anyway?' she grunted but Debbie was equal to that one.

'If you want to go to the disco, P.J. is arranging it,' she

announced importantly. 'And I'm the dance committee secretary and I take all the notes down.'

If that was the case, perhaps it would be better not to fall out with drippy Debbie so Jemma flashed her a huge smile and told her that P.J. had gone up the room they all went to when they wanted to be secret, right at the top of the Grove next to the little flight of stairs. She pointed at the window where she could see somebody's little white face peering out.

'Up there,' she said. 'Where that lad is.'

They all turned and looked and, as they did, the face just disappeared.

Fraser looked at her oddly. 'Don't you start,' he warned. 'It's bad enough having one of you flying round seeing ghosts.' Jemma didn't know what he was talking about and said so.

He bent closer to her. 'Listen,' he whispered. 'You'll have your Debbie terrified again. That's by where she said she saw you know who.'

'So what?' replied Jemma. 'Just because she's seeing things, it doesn't mean I am. I just saw somebody at that window. A little white face.'

They all turned and looked at the window again and a thought struck Fraser. The window Jemma was pointing at was in the old bit of the Grove and there was no way she could have seen anyone's face at it. He told her this and she demanded to know why. She knew what she'd seen but Fraser's next remark made even cocky little Jemma think twice.

'You didn't see anyone at that window,' said Fraser, holding up his hand when she tried to interrupt. 'You didn't,' he carried on, 'because that window is twelve feet off the ground and to get your face up that high you'd need to be on a ladder.'

Debbie was no help. She looked at Jemma with her eyes

dark and foreboding. 'Unless it was somebody, like, floating in the air,' she murmured. 'Floating, hanging. Floating.'

Jemma looked at her with irritation. Debbie revelled in being terrified and a lot of the time Jemma went along with it. Sometimes it was fun feeling tingly and scary. Not this time, though. She looked at the window again. She hadn't seen a ghost. She'd seen someone playing silly beggars and she intended to find out who it was and tell their fortune in no uncertain manner. Jemma didn't like being messed about. She stalked off, head high, tail wagging.

Speedy was unusually thoughtful as he climbed up the little stairs to the committee room. He was only half-listening to P.J. and Duncan who were discussing the number one topic of conversation, how to arrange the disco. He grunted from time to time to let them know he was still there but his stomach was turning over and it wasn't anything he had eaten.

Speedy's natural role in life, as he saw it, was as Robert's main protector, so his ego had taken a nasty battering when Robert met Charley and immediately rejected him. Speedy had never ever seen anyone go downhill quite as fast as that, not even on *Ski Sunday*. Robert had simply fallen head over conkers in love. Speedy couldn't see it, not for a minute. Girls were like the plague, according to Speedy, and to be avoided as such. Lou Gallagher had watched his outright disgust all the way through the love affair and had chuckled quietly more than once. 'Just you wait!' she thought to herself. 'Just you wait, my lad, till you catch it!' But people develop at different rates and Speedy hadn't yet entered the world of the hot flush, or experienced the feet-too-big syndrome of dancing and dating.

Now he was worried. It looked very much as if Robert might be weakening in his approach to Charley. He'd seen

76

him borrow some money off Lou and then heard him announce he was going to have a cup of coffee mid-morning in the Metro Centre. Speedy knew who he'd be having the coffee with. The one who'd started all the trouble. Why couldn't she just leave him alone, he moaned to Lou. The next thing anybody knew, Robert would stop going down the gym, stop exercising, and all his big ideas of getting fit and playing football again would get blown right out of the window just because of some stupid girl with golden hair and blue eyes and a shiny jacket.

Duncan turned and nudged P.J. Speedy was lost in his own thoughts.

He'd had a great idea just after Robert had left for the Metro Centre. He'd waited a bit and then casually drifted off after him, intending to butt in and make a nuisance of himself. Eventually, he reasoned, Charley would get the message and take herself off. He soon found the two ex-lovebirds and even from a distance it was pretty obvious that he wasn't going to have to do anything to make Charley drift off. Her head was down and, from Robert's tone of voice and gestures, it was only a matter of time before she got the big heave-ho. Speedy watched, entranced. He held his breath, and the Saturday morning Metro Centre crowd ebbed and flowed round him, until with a surge of glee he saw Charley walk off with her head down. Then the rest of the plan had come into operation. He casually sauntered across and sat down opposite the unusually subdued Robert. And then he noticed that she'd left her damn handbag as an excuse to come back. Well, Speedy wasn't going to fall for that one. He picked up the bag and shot off after the golden head.

But then it had all gone to pieces. He had called her name and she had turned round and all he could see was her face, beautiful and sad, with tears streaming down her cheeks. She had shaken her head, unable to say anything, and he had gone back to the table and laid into Robert, there and then, for making Charley cry. And now he couldn't get her or her sad, beautiful face out of his mind.

Lou would have said, told you so.

Speedy, in love, went into the committee room and sat on the floor. The other two lads looked at him.

'Flu, probably,' said P.J.

Duncan nodded. 'That, or cholera,' he said.

But Speedy was too far gone even to get the joke and they had to have the meeting without him. Without his mind, anyway, which wasn't necessarily a bad thing.

'OK,' Duncan said. 'I know there's no ghosts. You know there's no ghosts. We all know there are no such things as ghosts, right?'

They all nodded, and Duncan went on to say that even though there were no such things as ghosts, someone (or something, as Debbie had pointed out) was rollicking round the Grove at night, dropping candle wax and giving the general impression that there *are* such things as ghosts. This was beginning to have two effects on the potential party-going Byker Grove public: one, people wouldn't buy tickets because they didn't want to run into a screaming apparition; two, people wouldn't buy tickets for fear of being pounced on by someone who was nutty enough to want to be mistaken for a ghost. As Duncan finished, Speedy came out of an erotic daydream which featured him and a certain other party who he had just rescued from a horde of warlike savages and who was beginning to express her thanks in the customary manner.

He sniffed and was glad of the distraction. He had been beginning to get carried away and he knew his face was red because Duncan said so.

'What?' muttered Speedy.

P.J. sighed patiently. 'What are we going to do about it?' he said.

78

Speedy had no idea what he was talking about but covered for a bit until Duncan and P.J. ignored him again.

'We'll have to go looking for it,' said P.J. and Duncan snorted.

'Are you seeing Debbie Dobson?' he demanded. 'She's always going on about *it*. It's not an it, it's a person of some kind or another and it's going to ruin our disco unless we can get rid of it.' He was shouting loud enough now for even Speedy to get the general idea.

'Ghostbusters!' Speedy yelled, and they looked at him as if he'd finally flipped. But when he calmed down and they sieved through what he was saying, it really did seem to make some sense. Set traps, was Speedy's idea. Cotton stretched across doors, talcum powder sprinkled in empty rooms, hairs in chewing gum stuck across doorlocks – they'd soon find out if anyone was roaming the Grove at night. They looked at each other.

'And when we do find out,' P.J. said, 'what do we do, then?' The answer was obvious. When they found out who and what, in came the troops to find him or her or it and hand it over to the authorities. Speedy did sound just one note of caution. What if there *were* such things as ghosts, he wanted to know. People had once thought the earth wasn't round, now they knew it was. What if it was the same thing with ghosts? They told him that it wasn't the same thing and he nodded his head and got back to dreaming of Charley while the rest of them plotted when and how.

Then the door opened and in popped Jemma Dobson's cheery little face. She looked around the room, giving Duncan an especially warm smile. 'Where's our Debbie?' she said, coming right into the room.

Speedy lifted P.J.'s arm, looked at his armpit and then shook his head. 'She's not in her usual place, that's for sure,' he chortled and hooted when P.J. aimed a crack at his ear. Jemma looked a little puzzled.

'Why? What's up?' asked P.J., and Jemma, suddenly feeling a bit iffy about her sister's whereabouts, told them that Debbie had left half an hour before, to come up to the committee room. They all knew she was definitely not the kind of person who ought to be hanging round dark corridors and stairs. P.J. took charge.

'We'd better have a little look round,' he said quickly. 'Make sure she's all right.' And so they split into pairs, Jemma making sure she was with Duncan, and spreading the word as they went, so that very quickly the whole of Byker Grove was alive with kids looking for Debbie Dobson.

In the meantime, Geoff was receiving a small deputation consisting of Paul and Nicola. He had agreed that Paul could chat to the kids on green subjects but he also thought he should make sure that the lectures weren't going to be too far out. Paul had the true fanatic's gleam in his eye from time to time and there was never any harm in making sure. But as Geoff listened, he found himself charmed more and more by what Paul had to say. He had plans for a quiz and some prizes which he would supply, and he would get the kids started on thinking up ideas for Gaia to help herself. He explained the theory of Gaia as Mother Earth, a self-regulating entity (and Geoff thought privately that there were a couple of different things to consider ahead of that theory), but on the whole Paul made sense and Geoff was looking forward to hearing what he had to say. Then he listened, puzzled, to a mounting hubbub outside his office door and, going outside, found the place seething with excited kids.

He shouted for silence, asked what was going on, and was immediately told from a dozen different places that Debbie Dobson had disappeared, probably kidnapped by the ghost and dragged off to some dank dripping dungeon in the bowels of Byker Grove. He took Jemma and Duncan into his office and sat them down, asked carefully what they'd seen and tried to make some sense of it. He knew very well how over-active a lot of little imaginations could be and he knew very well the power of suggestion. But, as he looked at their sensible, stubborn faces, he became convinced that they certainly both believed they had seen something, whatever it was.

'And it wasn't anyone you recognised?' he asked. They shook their heads solemnly. 'You both know that Debbie thought she saw Gill, don't you?' he went on, but Jemma replied stoutly that Gill was dead and that she had seen somebody. Not a ghost, not something, but somebody. It was someone queer-looking all right, that much she conceded but it wasn't a figment of her imagination. Meanwhile, outside, to the sound of roaring, hooting Byker Grovers, Debbie was found. She'd wanted to go to the lavatory but, being Debbie, she'd gone to the one at home. (The Dobsons only live about a hundred yards away from the Grove and Debbie is a fairly fussy little girl.) Geoff shook his head and she looked at him indignantly. It was bad enough everybody knowing you'd been to the loo, she didn't need head-shaking as well.

Geoff calmed them all down and went into his office, taking Fraser in with him. He sat the lad down, talked at length about his worry that somebody was using the Grove for something unsavoury, and asked him to keep an eye out. Fraser nodded and went, mind still in turmoil about the proposed disco. He knew the others would be expecting him to help but he wasn't so sure he could now. Also, if there was one, he needed to make sure that Spuggie had something to wear.

Geoff looked at the telephone. He didn't want to start anything unnecessarily but he knew he had to get a bit of help from somewhere. He called Bob Grant (the community copper with special responsibility for the Grove) and asked if he could drop by. Grant agreed at once. There was something he needed to show Geoff anyway. Then all the Byker Grovers went home.

At ten o'clock, five of them came back and watched Geoff lock up the building. Then Duncan worked his magic with the picklocks and they went in and set all kinds of ghost traps. They chattered a lot in hushed voices, mainly out of nervousness.

They would have been a lot more nervous if they could have gone back in just after Duncan closed the door behind them, because somebody went and examined their traps with a great deal of interest.

The next day, of course, Geoff found more wax all over the Grove. He also got talcum powder on his shoes and black cotton caught in his moustache and found wedged gum in practically every door.

Bob Grant came over in the late afternoon, just before the kids came in, and Geoff welcomed him with a cup of tea. He looked with interest at what Grant had over his arm. From about fifty yards away, Nicola looked with more than interest. She looked with horror at the satchel she and Paul had used to carry the cards that had found their way on to more than fifty large cars the previous Saturday. She turned tail and ran down to the telephone box at the end of the drive, followed nosily by Donna who arrived just in time to hear the tail end of the conversation.

'I don't care!' Nicola was screaming. 'The police are here and they've got your bag. Stay away! You fool!' And she slammed the phone down to turn and see Donna with one eyebrow raised.

'That sounded exciting,' commented Donna. 'Come and do me hair and tell us all about you and the police and Paul.' Nicola fumed and nodded. She might just as well or Donna'd never stop talking about it.

Geoff didn't recognise the bag. Paul never used anything

that might be traced. Geoff did, however, show Grant the candle wax and all the other odd signs.

Grant looked at him strangely. 'There's an old chapel here, isn't there?' he asked.

Geoff nodded heavily. Grant had jumped to the same conclusion as him. It had been in all the papers a couple of weeks before – traces of black magic ceremonies had been found in a disused church up on the moors outside town. Geoff took Grant into the old chapel at the back of the Grove to show him the latest find. It was a bunch of chicken feathers, a half-burned red candle and some stains on the floor. Grant bent down to look closer. Then he looked up, his face changed.

'Someone's killed a chicken,' he said quietly and Geoff nodded.

'Problem is,' added Geoff, 'were they hungry or what?'

In the girls' lavatory, Nicola was staring with disbelief at the very attractive girl who had been directed in by a giggling Jemma to see her.

'What did you say?' she asked. The girl looked a trifle pained at Nicola's tone. Donna watched entranced. This was better than *Neighbours*.

The black girl started again. 'I just wondered if you could tell me where to find Paul Skerrett. Only, I've got a date with him here in about ten minutes.'

Nicola swept out like a yacht under full sail. And Debbie grinned at Tessa Awe, for that was the girl's name.

'Must have been something you said, honey,' grinned Donna. She patted the seat beside her. 'Sit down and tell us all about you and Paul.'

CHAPTER FIVE

The worst thing of all for Nicola was that the whole scene had been played out right in front of Donna. She had left the hated newcomer sitting there in the girls' loo WITH DONNA BELL, the Mouth of the North. If there had been a tale-telling Olympics, Donna would have been the champion, any distance, any weight, any discipline. Nicola cursed herself cold in her own bedroom while she wondered whether she should cut up Paul's photograph with her nail scissors or just rip it to pieces with her teeth. She did neither in the end, just took it out of her purse and threw it down the lavatory, rescuing it a second later and drying it on a tissue.

Actually she needn't have worried about Tessa Awe saying anything to Donna. Tessa took one look at Donna's expression, made up of roughly equal portions of malice and delight. Then she smiled sweetly and got the hell out of there. She also realised that she had put her foot in it up to the shoulders as far as the pretty kid with the dark hair and the soft eyes was concerned. It had been Paul's fault, of course. Lots of things were. She ought to have been told, though, that he had a girlfriend at Byker Grove. Then, maybe she wouldn't have put her foot in it. She went in search of him right away, found him down at the Metro Centre and told him what had happened. She didn't know what to expect. She certainly didn't expect him to throw back his head and roar with laughter.

'It wasn't funny,' she said. 'That kid was upset. I'd like to tell her the truth. What's her name, where can I find her?' He looked her straight in the eye and, even though she wasn't afraid of him, she knew when not to cross him.

'I'll take care of it,' he said, and when she pushed him a little, he got cross, stood up and walked off. But not before Donna, who had zoomed after Tessa, had observed the

84

whole scene and – considerate as ever – telephoned Nicola to bring her up to date. Nicola slammed the phone down, burst into tears and resolved to become a nun if they took Protestants.

Geoff and Bob Grant didn't know about any of this, of course, and they hadn't connected Paul, Nicola and the satchel, anyway. Geoff was still puzzled about the wax and the feathers but Grant did manage to set his mind at rest about the black magic stuff by making a phone call to the police station. It turned out that the whole thing had been started by a newspaper adding two and two together and getting eight hundred and thirty-four. It was just silly season journalism, made attractive by a photograph of the leggy farmer's daughter who had been around when the rumour broke in the first place. So they scratched that and Geoff told Grant about the black cotton and stuff. Grant nodded. It sounded to him as if Geoff was afflicted with a gang of amateur ghostbusters. It also occurred to him that there might be a gang of amateur ghosts. Geoff stared at him. He hadn't thought of that.

'Ah!' he mused. 'Hide and seek in the dark with illusions added. Right?'

Grant nodded. He also asked if anything had gone missing and they both came to the same conclusion. Somebody was playing silly beggars and if they didn't stop soon from boredom, Geoff would put something on the noticeboard that would make them stop.

Then Grant produced the other reason for a friendly community police visit. It was a large and lurid poster adorned with a skull and crossbones and a pompously worded warning about the dangers of joy-riding. Geoff winced and Grant sighed. This was the last thing in the world that Geoff wanted on the wall of Byker Grove so soon after Gill's death. He said so but then Grant trumped his ace. He pointed out that the police committee member who was pushing the poster was also the man tipped to be in control of youth club and ancillary funding for the next financial period. Grant had a very well-established network of informants all over his patch and he was usually right about these things. Geoff thought about it for quite a while before shaking his head.

'I canna do it,' he exclaimed. 'It's too soon after the accident. They're starting to forget but it's still too soon.'

Grant nodded sympathetically and promised to make soothing noises at the police station if there was any comeback.

Then he drove away, watched with interest by the gang of lads hiding on the roof and discussing the reasons for his visit. They needed to know because later that night they were going to set a fresh set of traps, Geoff having trampled all over the last lot with his great elephant feet. They didn't want any community coppers around, and they didn't want Debbie and Jemma there either.

You might just as well not want the sun to come up. There is a certain sort of sweet persistence which is very difficult to defend against, and the Dobson girls have it in abundance. They quietly amassed their best ghostbusting gear while Nicola lay in her bedroom with her head under the pillow pretending she was dead. Debbie looked scornfully at Jemma's idea of a top to wear in a secret situation. It was white and lacy and was bound to stand out. She told Jemma so, thus falling into the trap Jemma had set, and having to lend her the new one she'd only had about a week.

Later that night, they slid up to a darkened Grove, its black bulk just visible against the slightly lighter sky. The night was cold and clear and the stars twinkled while the two girls waited for P.J., Duncan and Speedy. They hadn't let

Fraser in on the secret, having also had doubts about where his loyalties would lie. P.J. and Speedy and Duncan made unconvincing owl noises till Jemma went down and told them to shut up. Then Duncan let them into the building and they went about their business.

This time they were a little more selective, only going into the mainly unused rooms and being a good deal more subtle, with no obvious cotton but a lot of matching of tiny little bits of sticky paper and, as well as that, Debbie wrote down exactly where they'd put each bit of paper. It took a long time but when they finally got out, they congratulated themselves on a job well done.

They didn't know about the eyes that watched all the way down the drive in the cold light of the now risen moon. The same eyes went directly to the only thing left behind that was really different from the last time and bent close to it, puzzled. It was a little battery-operated tape recorder. P.J. reasoned that this was the best way to find out if anyone was actually moving about at night. It was a nice piece of machinery, and very sensitive; sensitive enough to catch even the sound of light breathing, which was what it was doing.

The next day, Charley and Donna and Nicola were coming home from school together on the bus. Charley was carrying another red rose, the third one that had mysteriously appeared. This one was worse. It had been found with her name on it on the school doorstep and Charley had been treated to some very heavy sarcasm from the Head about pop stars and heart-throbs. The Head was a royal pain in the bum, anyway, and never missed a chance to put somebody down, especially somebody whose clothes weren't exactly dropping off their matchstick-thin legs and arms and whose parents could afford to do a bit more than buy gruel twice a week. Middle-class kids with rosy cheeks weren't worthy of his attention, especially middle-class kids with rosy cheeks and secret admirers who bought them expensive flowers. He had toyed with the idea of throwing the flower away but, like a lot of bullies, he was also a coward and not sure of the legal position. Also, the school was thinking of opting out and Mr and Mrs Charlton might end up on the Board of Governors and who knew where that might lead. So he gave Charley the flower and a shovelful of heavy wit. She wished he had thrown it away. She wished she'd thrown it away herself as soon as Donna started digging her claws in.

'It is romantic, mind, isn't it?' purred Donna and Charley answered back like a shot. Romantic it certainly was not. It was creepy. She felt as if somebody was watching her and licking his lips. It was horrible.

Nicola saw that she was really upset. 'Maybe it's Robert,' she suggested but Charley shook her head. 'Maybe he's changed his mind and doesn't know how to say so,' Nicola persisted. 'Lads are like that. They can't talk about anything,' she went on and was sorry at once. She recognised that look in her alleged best friend's eye.

'Well, *you* ought to know all about lads,' said Donna in honeyed tones. 'By the way,' she pretended to remember, 'how's that lad, whatsisname, Paul, the one with the black girlfriend? How's he? You used to see him, didn't you? But I notice he hasn't been around much lately.'

Nicola got off the bus and Charley looked at Donna. She genuinely couldn't understand what made Donna do things like that to her supposed best friend. Donna just shrugged. She did what she felt like, always had. Anyway, it was time Nicola snapped out of it and stopped mooning about. It was quite obvious to anyone with an ounce of sense that Paul Skerrett had given Nicola the soldier's farewell and she ought to start talking to her friends again.

They got off the bus together and Donna wheedled the rose off Charley who'd been planning to put it in the bin anyway.

Donna thought she could probably make some mischief with it and walked along, happy as a pig in muck, rolling the possibilities around her fertile brain. Charley was standing there uncertainly, not keen to spend any more time than she had to with Donna, when a car rolled up beside her and a face she thought she'd never see again poked out of the driver's window. The face was large as life and twice as ugly and grinning as if sure of his welcome, which was a prime piece of cheek because he'd been sacked from the Grove for, in Geoff's opinion, endangering the morals of a minor. The grin was especially cheeky because the minor had been Charley. But, in spite of all that, he got a grin back because it was hard to hate Dexter Dutton. Charley knew, even if Geoff didn't, that Dexter had never put a foot wrong when dealing with her and Hayley, or a hand, either.

'Haway, Charlesworth!' shouted Dexter, as he got out of the car and gave her a swift hug. He was dressed in the very height of fashion – soft leather trousers, bright red silk shirt and a fringed jacket that must have cost a bob or two, as her father was fond of saying. Dexter gave her a bit of a twirl to show off the threads and gave her another grin which made her feel quite good, in spite of the depression she was in. But she still tightened her lips against the smile.

'All right,' said Charley coolly. 'What do you want this time, Dexter?'

He was mock hurt but still grinning. 'Is that nice?' he said in pained tones. 'You meet your oldest friend in showbiz who gave you your biggest chance ever and all you can say is, what do you want? Charming!'

Charley grimaced, remembering the chance she had had until the rat-smooth medallion man, Steve Rettega, had sold her and her song right down the river. All her problems, Robert's neck and all, had flowed direct from that song and that record.

Dexter, also remembering, fell silent himself, then skilfully changed the subject. 'Your mate Hayley's doing all right,' he offered. 'With big bad Vaz Takedeli, I hear. Blue beat and bouncin' hips for little Hayley!'

Charley asked him if he just wanted to gloat or was there something she could help him with? Hayley had been her singing partner – only she had come out of the affair with a career in clubs and an older man. Charley had been left with first a crippled boyfriend and, now, none at all.

Then Dexter hit a serious note. He gave her his card, black and gold, embossed with music motifs. She nearly gave it back, it was so similar to Rettega's, same flash, no style. But, suddenly thinking of something, she tapped the card on her teeth and listened to Dexter's sales pitch.

To be fair to Dexter, it wasn't just a sales pitch. He had introduced her to Rettega, who had behaved like the rat Dexter had hoped he wasn't. Rettega had taken Charley for a ride, using her to make a demo disc for almost nothing, only releasing it in the North-East and selling it to a major voice in the States. Dexter felt a bit responsible, especially when he saw the little blue stains under Charley's eyes and realised that she looked really unhappy, as well as a good deal older and wiser. Which wasn't exactly a good thing in a kid that age.

'You were born to sing, Charley,' declared Dexter, remembering the glorious sounds he'd heard all those months ago in the sleazy little club by the river when she had opened her throat like a blackbird and let all the joy inside her flood out. 'You were born to sing and you were just handled wrong and the number stank. You give me a ring as soon as you feel like singing again.'

She was pert and told him not to hold his breath but he took it the right way because he saw just the tiniest glimmer of interest in her eyes and he thought maybe she wasn't a lost cause after all. Charley watched him drive off, and put the card away very carefully. Just then, all the others who had been watching open-mouthed, ran up, Speedy in the lead. He'd just seen who she'd been talking to and he was so cross he was spitting feathers.

'Who was that?' he asked angrily even though he knew. Charley looked at him, not knowing what was churning round inside him, of course. She told him it had been Dexter and was astonished by his reaction.

'Him that got sacked from the Grove? Keep away from him!' shouted Speedy. 'Have nothing to do with him!'

'No!' said Jemma, sticking her oar in. (If Jemma grows up, she will make the University Boat Race team.) They all stared at her.

'You've never even heard of Dexter Dutton,' Debbie told her sister scathingly.

Jemma was unconcerned. Not only had she heard of him, she knew the band he managed, the Swift Snakes, and the style of music they played, rockabilly. She left the assembled throng looking amazed, and sauntered off, well pleased.

Speedy took up the cudgels again. He announced that he was going to tell Geoff that Dexter had been hanging round the Grove, having been specifically forbidden to do so on pain of losing all his front teeth. Charley frowned.

'I'd rather you didn't, please, Speedy,' she said in a soft voice which the others didn't hear. Speedy was thrown all of a heap. He couldn't refuse her anything, not when she looked at him like that.

'But why?' he stuttered. 'He's a bad fellow, him, taking you and Hayley down the Riverfront,' but she looked at him pleadingly, and he was gone, lost.

Back at the foster home, Lou Gallagher sat with a worried look on her face and a blue airmail envelope on the kitchen table. She picked it up and examined if for the umpteenth time that day. It was addressed to Joanne and there were a number of things about it that made Lou excited, gloomy and scared all at the same time. It was clear that it had come from America, even clearer that it had military connections, and clearer still that it was going to blow Joanne's fragile and unnatural self-control to pieces. Fraser was the first one back from school, followed by Robert, Spuggie, Joanne and Speedy. Fraser, watchful as ever, saw Lou whisk the letter out of sight, and he increased his speed out through the hall and up to his bedroom. She let him go, but about half an hour later stopped him, just as they were all off to the Grove.

She sat him down in the kitchen, showed him the letter and asked him what he'd been doing. He just shrugged and pointed out that it was addressed to Joanne, not him. She didn't get cross, just practical. She knew perfectly well that Joanne would never have written to the United States and therefore it was unlikely that anyone would have written to her, unprompted. Fraser nodded and thought for a second, picking at the cloth.

Then he looked up, straight into Lou's eyes, and said, unrepentant, 'I thought she should have a chance to get in touch with her dad.'

Lou shook her head, angry now. 'You took a lot on yourself, Fraser. A lot,' she said, with emphasis. 'What if she doesn't want to have anything to do with him? What if he doesn't want to have anything to do with her? What if it all just leads to more heartbreak for Joanne?'

Fraser's lips tightened. 'When they both know all the facts, they'll be able to decide,' he pointed out. 'If I hadn't done it, they might have gone through their whole lives without being given the chance to decide.'

His firm statement ended the conversation, and Lou went up to put the letter on Joanne's bed. Then she thought better of it, took the letter down with her again, picked up the telephone and asked Geoff to send Joanne home as quickly as possible without alarming her. Then she made herself a cup of tea against the coming storm.

The band of trainee ghostbusters bubbled along the road and into the drive leading to the Grove. The air of anticipation was so thick and juicy you could have cut it with a knife. They were about to listen to the tape recorder they had cunningly placed in the spookiest part of the building to see if they really did have a night-time visitor. They weren't saying much, hoping not to call attention to themselves, not realising that a bunch of kids, mouths tight shut, cheeks red and eyes sparkling with suppressed excitement is about as hard to miss as a black cat on an iceberg. Geoff saw them as he looked out of the window and immediately thought, trouble, but then his and their attention was shifted quickly and surprisingly. Alison drove up, looked at the Grove, and disappeared inside.

Alison had decided that the only way to get on with her life was to get on with it. A woman without a man is like a fish without a bicycle. That was going to be Alison's motto from now on. Geoff hid a little grin. He knew his Alison and, even from that distance, he could almost read her mind. Good on you, mate, he thought to himself and went out to meet her. He gave her a swift squeeze and held her away.

'Would *you* give up?!' she said.

'Never,' answered Geoff and grinned again. 'And nor have you, have you?'

Alison shook her head back and told him that life was for living. He wanted to know what she would be doing about the house and she told him that too – living in it, paying the mortgage and doing it up, as planned. There would be one element missing, of course, but it wasn't an element that was necessary to Alison's future and it could damn well please itself. And it wasn't getting its half of the deposit back either.

Then she went back to work and endured a couple of hours of very heavy sympathy from Mary O'Malley, combined with some tea and a piece of home-made parkin that Mary just happened to have about her person. Mary O'Malley was a great believer in the restorative powers of home-made cakes and doled them out on every possible occasion.

In the committee room the gang's business nearly stopped before it started. For Geoff suddenly came into the room and P.J. only just managed to hide the tape recorder. Joanne was sent home and Spuggie volunteered to go with her. Fraser saw them leave and thought hard. He couldn't let her walk into the letter cold, so he ran after the two girls and told Joanne what he had been doing.

She couldn't believe it, just stood there with her mouth open and her heart dropping down through the bottom of her stomach. After all she'd been through over the last two years with her supposed brother, the waiting and the hoping and final heartbreak when he had just turned out to be a fake, for Fraser to do what he had done was almost beyond belief.

What Fraser had done, was to read in a newspaper that a law had been passed in America which said orphans who suspected that their fathers had been US servicemen would be given every possible help to trace such fathers. He had then got in touch with Joanne's lawyer, the one who had tried to help with her supposed brother, and he had told Fraser where to write. Fraser had written a simply worded letter, telling Joanne's story. What he didn't know was that Joanne's father had been engaged in the same long search. He had tried, after the war, to send money for Joanne's mother, not knowing that she was pregnant, only knowing, too late, that not only had she died, she had also had a little girl who might well have been his. At present, all Joanne knew was that Fraser had put her in line for more sadness and disappointment.

'He won't want to see me!' she screamed. 'Who'll want a

half-caste child turning up after all these years? He'll be married, he'll have children of his own. How's it going to make me feel when he writes and sends me money and tells me to clear off? How?' She burst into tears. And Spuggie put her arms round the shaking shoulders and looked sadly at Fraser over Joanne's head. He'd really put his foot in it this time. But Fraser just carried on mildly, saying that Joanne didn't know anything at all about what to expect. What she had to do was go home and read the letter and then decide. She couldn't decide anything until she had read the letter. Joanne flew at him then and kicked him on the leg. Fraser hopped about for a bit, thinking grimly to himself that doing good wasn't all that it was cracked up to be. Then he went back to the Grove. And Joanne and Spuggie went home, because the Grove was certainly no place for Joanne, not till her puffy eyes had gone down a bit; not with Donna Bell around, anyway.

In the committee room, they set the tape recorder running. It had a two-hour tape in and they settled down and listened. And listened and listened and listened and listened. Nothing. Not a dicky bird.

'The tape's no good,' said Speedy, in disgust. He was always the one who lost patience quickest.

'Speedy!' said Jemma. 'Stop it!'

Speedy looked round, hurt. He couldn't stop – he wasn't doing anything.

'That tapping,' said Jemma again. 'Stop the tapping.' They all listened and P.J. turned to the others, holding out his hand, palm down, for quiet. They were absolutely silent as he pointed to the tape recorder and slowly turned it up. The tapping was coming from the recorder. Only it wasn't tapping and it soon became quite loud and then faded again.

'What was that?' said Debbie, her eyes round and fearful. They all shook their heads.

'Listen carefully, this time,' said Speedy and bent his head close to the little whirring machine. 'It's coming back.'

It was and they listened as the sound came right up to the recorder and they suddenly all recognised it as footsteps. But nobody said anything as they listened with breath stopped and hearts trying to burst out through their chests. Then another low and almost imperceptible sound started. They listened carefully.

'It's the wind,' Jemma exclaimed. And they all nodded, except Debbie who looked at her scornfully. It had been dead still that night, no wind, she told them. And they remembered and listened harder. Debbie got it this time.

'It's breathing,' she whispered. 'It's something breathing right into the recorder. It must have its mouth right up against the mike. Like a – '. She stopped.

Speedy finished her sentence. It could have been a werewolf, he said, and looked round for approval. P.J. shook his head sadly and nodded towards Debbie who had gone green.

Speedy tried to backtrack. 'No. If it had been a werewolf, it would probably have gnashed its teeth,' he said reassuringly.

'What's it doing now?' asked Duncan. It sounded as if it was gnashing something but before Debbie could disappear shrieking out of the window, the thing did something a lot more horrible. It laughed. It was not a nice laugh. It was the kind of laugh the mad scientist does just before he cuts someone up or the kind of laugh the living dead zombie does just before it bursts through the door and gets the teenage babysitters. P.J. reached out and switched it off quickly. He wasn't scared, of course, but it was his tape recorder and he didn't want anybody nervous coming past and being frightened out of their wits. They all nodded wisely when he said this. Very sensible, they agreed. Then they looked back at the recorder and Duncan said what everybody else was thinking.

'Nobody would want to go to a party where you might run into something laughing like that,' he announced.

They shook their heads. Anybody who laughed like that would be a very definite party-wrecker, worse than a skinhead setting fire to the curtains (which had happened over on the Poulton estate just before Christmas the year before). The door to the committee room eased open slowly and Fraser peered in (he was there as the new part-time helper). He looked at the small faces, made smaller by doubt and fright.

'What's up with you lot?' he asked. P.J. didn't say anything. He rewound a bit of the tape and let it play. Fraser listened. Then he looked at them again and gestured P.J. to turn it off. They explained that they'd hoped to set a trap to catch whoever or whatever it was playing silly beggars and the trap seemed to have worked better than they would have liked.

Fraser thought about it. He has an analytical brain. He is also slightly more advanced than other lads his age, having spent a couple of years being the father, effectively, of the Campbell household. He could see the problem from both sides. Part of the success of Byker Grove was that it was very different from youth clubs, as such. There was no doing good just for the sake of doing good. There was swearing in moderation, eyes were averted discreetly over dark corner snogging and the kids were generally allowed to work things out for themselves. They knew the penalties if things went wrong. Because of all this, they behaved very well, on the whole, even if none of them were exactly plaster saints. The dance was a good idea. It was slightly naughty, as all the best schemes are, but there was no evil in it. Fraser had an idea, too, about how it could be effectively policed without any of the partygoers knowing. But they certainly couldn't have a party if they had a mad, laughing lodger in the attic. There had to be a way of getting rid without causing a major fuss.

He suddenly wondered about something. How had they all got in? Duncan produced his picklocks, smiling weakly. Fraser shook his head, cross. 'What would happen,' he asked, 'if we had a real break-in and somebody shopped you, Duncan, for having that lot?' They all looked at each other, indignant, until Fraser asked them how many people besides themselves they had sort of, possibly, maybe mentioned the party to. There were two or three red faces at this and Fraser nodded. Enough said. If they did anything further, it would be done through channels. A particular channel, called Fraser, as it happened. The committee held a swift and silent meeting, agreed, and that was that.

Then they went on with the more important stuff, like who would be wearing what and what kind of music would go down well. P.J. had recently got an advance copy of a session by Half Man Half Biscuit and anyone who wanted to could check it out, he said. They went down to the games room and put it on the machine, turned down very low, and listened to it, creased up. They had one nasty scare on the Fred Titmus track which has to be played fairly loud to be appreciated properly. Mary O'Malley came out of the kitchen and heard the chorus but obviously didn't believe her ears and disappeared again. Jemma said she didn't think much of it and who was Fred Titmus anyway? But Duncan, P.J. and Speedy nearly had heart attacks laughing and so it went straight on the playlist.

Joanne and Spuggie got home and walked straight into Lou and the letter from America. Joanne didn't even open it. She snatched it out of Lou's fingers, ripped it in two and threw it into the empty fireplace.

'If you want to stop being my mother,' cried Joanne, 'all you have to do is say. But I'm happy with things the way they are.'

Then she took Spuggie off upstairs to learn how to play chess. Lou took the letter out of the fireplace and tucked it into her apron pocket. No matter what, Joanne was going to be given every chance to meet her father.

Winston was trying to get hold of Julie in London to ask her for another picture of Gill but didn't have enough money even to get the question out. He saw Kelly watching him sadly as he put the phone down.

'Do you think I'm stupid?' he asked and she shook her head. She did think, though, that he ought to get down to the Grove more and talk to his mates. While he was still thinking about this, the lurcher from the gypsy camp suddenly ran up behind him and knocked him over in delight. Then it sat there, looking really proud of itself. Winston had to laugh, looking at its stupid face. Also, it gave them something to do.

They chased the dog, caught it and took it over to where the trailers were. Kelly watched Winston with the lurcher and the seed of a little idea began to grow. His face was as happy as she had ever seen it as the three of them bounced along. But when they got to Mrs Finney's van, it was silent and deserted, and they got the fright of their lives when a man came up to them, unsmiling, cradling a shotgun, and just took the dog without saying a word. They came away as quickly as they could, not saying anything until they were well clear of the dark, eerie wood.

At the foster home, Lou took the letter out of her pocket and made a telephone call quickly before she changed her mind. Then she sat down and cried her eyes out, terrified but knowing that she'd had to do it.

Meanwhile, the roller coaster ride that was Nicola's love life took another sickening surge. She was quite enjoying her deep decline and had started to admire the very romantic dark shadows under her eyes. In fact she'd even helped them on a little with some eyebrow pencil. Then she walked round a corner and slap into Paul's grin. She tried to walk round him but Paul doesn't let people walk round him. He just held her by the upper arms so she couldn't move, then asked her why she wouldn't talk to him on the phone, and why she wouldn't see him. She told him in a few short sentences. Nobody two-timed her, not even Paul. He looked at her as if she was mad and then his face cleared.

'Ah!!' he grinned. 'Tessa told me you were upset. It's just a pity you didn't talk to me and let me tell you the truth.'

She waited, and what he said next made her heart drop like a stone. He told her that he and Tessa lived together and that they were all going to talk this through. And he took her home.

His smile should have prepared her for a succession of shocks. First, he lived in a vicarage. Second, Tessa was someone who lived with Paul and his dad while she finished her studies. Third, Paul loved Nicola and was never going to let her go. He put his arm round her on the settee and Tessa said she would love to stay and watch but she had a tennis lesson. Paul set out to woo Nicola all over again but, to tell the truth, he didn't have to try very hard and Nicola spent the best ever afternoon of her young life so far. In a vicarage front room, too, with a budgie watching. Then Paul lay with his head in her lap, and, slowly, expertly, talked her into doing what he had recruited her for in the first place.

'People who attack fur shops have done the Brigade a favour. All we have to do is show people who drive big cars that we can do the same to them and their cars and their garages. We don't actually have to do it, just show them that we could if we wanted to.'

Nicola stirred a little uncomfortably and he looked deep into her eyes again and she knew she'd do anything for him, no matter what. He knew it too, but the smile inside wasn't nearly as fetching as the one he showed the world. He looked at his watch. It was time, he said.

He took her over to the creepy magic shop in Backleigh where the shopkeeper gave them a very special package and Paul told her exactly what she had to do with it. She was terrified but he held her close and told her to trust him, he would never let her do anything bad. To her eternal sorrow, she did trust him and her life was never the same again.

Lou jumped a mile when the telephone rang. She nervously gave the man on the other end detailed instructions about how to get to Newcastle, put the telephone down and cried again. The die was cast now.

And a large, low, stretch limousine pulled up at the door of the Grove. It had tinted glass windows and the entire population gathered round and peered in. They backed off quite quickly when the door opened and a man only slightly smaller than Arnold Schwarzenegger got out and looked round slowly.

'Miss Campbell?' he asked and they all shook their heads, forgetting about Spuggie. All except Joanne who flew off and reappeared with the flame-haired urchin. The man's face softened into what might have been a smile and he bent down and pulled a large expensive-looking parcel out of the car, handing it to the puzzled little girl. Then his words made sense and her face shone like the sun on a spring morning.

'For the white queen,' he said. 'From the black king.' Nobody except Spuggie had the faintest idea what he was talking about and they all raced after the car, hooting and

CHAPTER SIX

Bill Paul knew that he was one of the luckiest guys in the world. His dad had died when he was eight or nine. He couldn't remember how old – it was as if his brain had resolutely drawn a line round that part of his life and declared it off limits. He had grieved for many a long day, he knew that, and his mother had been everything to him all that time. After a while she had met a man and had brought him home once or twice. Bill hadn't wanted to understand what was going on. He'd been about thirteen. He would go to his room when the big hero from Vietnam walked through the door and kissed his mother as if he had a right to. Bill stole money from his mother's purse so she would know how bad he felt and he dropped a couple of grades at school quite deliberately. He tried to start smoking but it made him so ill he had to forget it. He also drank a whole bottle of something blue and sweet but that just spurted straight out again all over his best baseball jacket.

Then the tall ex-soldier with the deep lines in the sides of his face caught him one day in the house when Mom wasn't home. He'd tried to get out, go upstairs, in the yard, anywhere. But Danny Paul – that was the man's name – wouldn't let him. He just sat Bill down on the swing by the back porch and talked to him. He told him he knew how he felt, told him that feelings like that were OK and natural and asked his permission to marry his mother. Bill didn't have to answer right away but Danny and Bill's mother both felt he ought to have a say in who he spent the rest of his life with.

The rest, folks, is history, as they say. His name is now Bill Paul and he has two little sisters, one of whom he has met, the other he is going to meet, although she doesn't know it yet. Danny Paul has told Bill about Joanne, the daughter he didn't know he had. Bill is at London University, studying for an extra qualification. And now he's on his way to New-castle upon Tyne, eating British Rail bacon and eggs and looking at green fields and toy villages and cows that look as if they've been designed specifically to go with little thatched cottages.

The plan has been hatched over the telephone with a nice-sounding lady, Miz Lou Gallagher. Bill is going to ease himself into his new sister's life and see if he can persuade her to come back with him, first to London where his dad and the rest of the family will say hello, then to Foster City built on the lagoons just south of San Francisco and, to Bill, the nearest thing to heaven in the whole wide world. Bill is fairly whole-hearted about things. Besides which he comes from California and Californians are very special people. The train rattled high over a picturesque town and stopped at the station, Durham. Bill sighed and gathered his bags together. Not far to go now. Zero hour and, for all his self-confidence and his smile and the remnants of his sun tan, he felt himself hoping, really hoping, that Joanne would like him.

The train sat outside Newcastle on a very high bridge over the river and he gathered his thoughts as he looked down at the water riffling in the wind. No ships, no docks any more, not much industry, but he had read about Newcastle upon Tyne and he knew it was a place with a very clear sense of itself, and that the people knew who they were too. He looked forward to making their acquaintance. The train finally shuddered and snorted and tugged its way into the station, and he got off with the sense of a journey starting rather than ending.

A comfortable, worried-looking woman stared at him and put her hand out. He smiled at her.

'Mr Paul?' she asked and he laughed out loud.

'No, mam, that's my father!' he replied. 'I'm Bill Paul. You must be – '

She supplied the answer with relief not just because he was

the right man but because he looked so nice. Lou was starting to feel she'd done the right thing after all, as they went outside to catch a bus and start plotting Joanne's future.

The plan was simple. Bill was to arrive at the Grove to do a project about young people's meeting-places. Only Geoff and Fraser would be in on the secret and Bill would just naturally get to know Joanne. Simple! (The plan did hit a slight snag, though. Spuggie saw him first and fell in love with him. But we'll talk about that later.) Lou took him round to a friend of hers, who ran a bed and breakfast place. This tickled Bill pink. He learned something new every day and bed and breakfast was so British he couldn't believe it. He also couldn't believe the size of the breakfast or the very small amount it was going to cost.

The following day was one the North-East might have specially arranged as a welcome for Bill. It was bright and clear but not as bright and clear as the blue eyes of the young girl who pointed him in the right direction when his street map turned out to be upside down. It was Charley herself who was coincidentally humming an American song when Bill came up and spoke to her.

'Excuse me,' said the deep brown voice and she spun round and smiled. 'Hi!' said Charley and the smile that came with the eyes and the greeting strengthened Bill's favourable impression of the North-East. She looked at the address and grinned again, saying she was going there herself. They walked together, chatting on the way, Charley darting little glances at Bill and Bill looking rather more openly at Charley.

As they came up the drive, it was as if someone had turned a searchlight on them. Conversations halted, eyes went round, and Spuggie nearly fell off the climbing frame.

'Look!' Jemma said to Donna.

'Oh, my word,' exclaimed Donna. 'That's very hunky, isn't it? I wonder if Charley needs a hand?' And she took off at a fast trot in the general direction of the newcomer. Jemma shook her head. Man-mad, Donna was. Man-mad.

Donna reached the front door just as Charley was pointing Bill towards Geoff's office. She jumped straight in and asked to be introduced but Bill just looked at her and eased past into the Grove with a big smile and a muttered apology, leaving Donna wondering what had happened.

Then Jemma arrived, genuinely curious as to what had gone wrong with Donna's sex appeal. Jemma likes to keep tabs on these things for future reference. In fact she even has a little book of notes about what to do when certain things happen in relationships. (If her mother ever finds it, there will be tears before bedtime!) Donna looked at her with distaste and asked why she didn't join the Brownies. Jemma said she'd sooner learn about lads than woods and trees, which made Donna grin a little. She grinned a bit more when Jemma carried on to say that she and Debbie were picking up quite a few tips by listening to Paul and Nicola having a whale of a time in the front room; they were at it like knives every chance they could get.

Donna grinned again. It wasn't the first time she'd thanked her lucky stars that she didn't have any little sisters.

Inside the Grove, Geoff took stock of Bill. Like most people, he liked the look of him, and listened to what he had to say with interest. Geoff had been worrying about Joanne for quite some time. She had been going to great pains recently to make herself look utterly Western, changing her hairstyle, using eye make-up to tone down the little hint of a tilt which made her eyes so attractive. He still had his doubts about what Bill intended to do, though, and he was blunt as ever.

'You have some idea, I suppose, of the damage you could do?' he asked, and Bill nodded. That was why he wanted to do it this way. If there was any danger to Joanne and her peace of mind, any danger at all, Bill would just disappear into the night as though he had never been.

He also wanted to meet Fraser, who he imagined was one hell of a guy. Geoff sent for him. Then he looked at Bill doubtfully again.

'You're not going to tell him who you are, surely?' he said. 'That's a hell of a load for a young fellow to carry.' But, from what Bill had heard, he reckoned that Fraser's shoulders were broad enough, no problem.

This was confirmed when Fraser came in, looking very calm and composed, and nodded quietly at Bill. In the middle of this, Spuggie bounced in, took one look at Bill, and fell head over heels, hook, line and sinker. 'Hello,' she said breathlessly. 'My name's Spuggie. You can call us Kirstie if you like. What's your name?' Bill smiled and Spuggie's year was complete – a computer chess player and a man to worship had all come along just at the right time. 'Do you play chess?' she whispered. If he didn't, he could soon learn. She'd teach him. She was still looking full in his eyes as Geoff manoeuvred her out through the door. Fraser apologised for his sister. Bill said he thought she was sweet and Geoff and Fraser snorted. Spuggie was a lot of things, they agreed, but sweet wasn't high on the list.

Then they worked out a plan of action. Bill was just to be seen round the building, to listen, to observe and to decide what ought to be done. Fraser nodded. He offered to give Bill the Grand Tour, introduce him round and, that way, include Joanne without being too obvious.

This they did and Spuggie produced Joanne as if she was her own creation, not realising the effect this would have on Bill. He could see Danny's cheekbones hiding in Joanne's little face and it made his voice skip just slightly as he said hello. Fraser turned away quickly, anxious not to give Bill away. He needn't have worried. Bill could have turned into a gibbering idiot and Spuggie would still have said he was wonderful.

Joanne liked him too. She couldn't have said why but there was something about him, even if he *was* American (and she was off all Americans at the moment). She would have tossed her long black hair at Bill, but he was already walking along the top landing.

Spuggie saw her look. 'I saw him first,' she said.

Fraser leaned back over the landing. 'No, you never,' he replied. 'Charley saw him first and Donna saw him next.' Spuggie didn't bat an eye. She'd seen him before Joanne and that was all that mattered. Then she had a great idea.

'Hey! Bill!' she shouted up. 'Do you want to see a really hellish chess computer?' He nodded and came back down the stairs.

Spuggie started to pull him away but he held back a little and asked Joanne why she didn't come too. She smiled sweetly and Spuggie looked daggers, but the three of them walked off together, the best of friends already.

Fraser watched them go and felt Geoff join him. The pair of them stood there, as if they were modelling toby jugs. This looked as if it might turn out very well indeed. They turned and congratulated each other. Then Geoff remembered something he had been worrying about.

'What about this disco everybody was so keen on?' he asked. 'That all seems to have gone very quiet all of a sudden. I hope there's nothing going on behind my back.'

Fraser shook his head. 'I'm working on it,' he said. 'But I may have to ask you for a bit of help nearer the time, all right?'

Geoff nodded. Already he trusted Fraser a lot more than he'd ever trusted Brad. Brad always wanted the kids to like him. Fraser didn't care who liked him, he just got on with the job. He rushed up the stairs two at a time just as P.J. and the others came round the corner in the opposite direction.

Jemma ended up as the meat in a lad sandwich for the first time ever, but she wasn't that impressed.

'What's up?' asked Fraser. P.J. put a finger to his lips and jerked his head until Fraser followed him into the committee room with the rest of the Wild Bunch. Then he listened to P.J.'s plan which he thought sounded quite good, providing it was done properly and providing it also had someone responsible masterminding it. He looked over the assembled talent and shook his head. P.J. would be needed on the technical gear, Speedy was too harum scarum and Duncan wasn't big enough in case they got into trouble.

His audience looked at him anxiously. 'I'll go inside this time and I'll unlock the door too. I don't want you bringing them picklock things this time, Duncan.' He warmed to his theme. 'I suppose you know, if a copper caught you with them things, you could end up inside?'

Duncan nodded dubiously. He hadn't actually thought about it but Fraser was making sense – no point getting done for nothing. He resolved to leave them at home for once.

Debbie and Jemma decided to leave the plotters for the time being. They were only going to talk about boring old technical stuff and they wanted to make sure they had enough ghostbusting gear and wash their hair and do all the things lads would never do, no matter where they were going. Nicola would be out, as well, and they could go through her wardrobe and see if there was anything worth nicking for the evening.

Nicola *was* out. She was out, turning cold on top of a bus that was going past a garage that sold big cars. Not that it would be selling many big cars in the foreseeable future. There had been the mother and father of all fires at this particular garage. The fire engines had gone and now it was all being cleared up. Nicola felt herself flooding with horror and fright.

She stood up and tried to look back at the garage but the bus went round a corner and people started to look at her curiously. She ran downstairs and jumped off the bus, falling heavily in her panic and banging into the wall. She picked herself up quickly, her arm grazed and blood beginning to ooze, but she was too panicky to do anything about it. She started to charge round the corner but stopped when she saw a couple of women gazing at her strangely. She half smiled at them, remembering Paul's rule. Smile! Don't be furtive. But all the rules went right out of her head when she finally did get round the corner and the full enormity of what had happened lay right in front of her.

It was much worse than it had seemed from the top of the bus. The whole of the car showroom was burned out and the shells of huge cars stood in pools of filthy water. She just stood and stared until she became aware that somebody was looking directly at her through the filthy glass window. It was the garage owner. She knew it was the garage owner because she had flirted with him a little the day before when she had been looking idly round the car showroom. She had told him she was waiting for her dad. She had needed an excuse, you see, to get into the showroom – the showroom where all the big cars were now burned out and useless – to leave behind the little parcel which Tyrone and Paul had assured her was only a joke. It was just to prove that the Green Brigade could plant a bomb anywhere, at any time, and there was no defence. Paul and Tyrone had shown her that the parcel only contained a timing device and a note, saying just that, and telling the garage man not to sell such wasteful cars. The same garage man who was even now looking at Nicola and talking urgently into the telephone.

She ran away as fast as her legs could carry her and started to look for Paul. She didn't have any luck, though, because Paul was no longer in Newcastle. Paul was in London, doing other things, a long way from the garage and Nicola, who was beginning to feel, with a terrible wave of hopelessness, that she had been used to commit a really serious crime. There was only one place to go and that was home, to explain things to her mum and dad. They'd get her out of it. She hadn't done anything, really. She hadn't known there was anything wrong with the parcel. Tyrone must have cheated her and Paul, for reasons of his own. If she could just get hold of Paul ... She telephoned again and got Tessa, whose voice went very guarded as she told Nicola that Paul was away and she didn't know where.

Nicola banged the telephone down and ran off, round the corner and into her own road, head down, terrified. She looked up only just in time. Her mother was at the door. Normally this would have been a comfort, but PC Grant was also at the door, and her mother was looking anxious. Nicola shrank back against the hedge, squeezing herself out of sight until Grant got in his car and went off down the road, and then another dreadful thought struck her. How much sympathy would she get from her mum and dad if the policeman had already told them that their darling daughter was about to be arrested for arson? Like most respectable working-class families in Newcastle, the Dobsons were very upright. They would have her down at the police station quicksticks, if only to explain. And where would that leave Paul?

She looked round frantically, nearly at the limit of her endurance. She seemed to have been running for hours since she'd got off the bus. Looking at her watch, she was startled to see that it had only been about twenty minutes. She breathed out slowly and tried to think rationally. She had to get a message to Paul but she couldn't leave a message with anyone without telling them what it was. What she had to do was go to the vicarage and leave a note in a sealed envelope with Tessa. Which meant that she had to get paper and stuff like that. She couldn't go home. The only other place was the Grove – she set off again at a fast clip.

At the Grove, Speedy and P.J. and Duncan were looking at a very queer piece of jiggery-pokery. It looked for all the world like a long, thin sword except that it wasn't sharp. It was attached to a pair of earphones. P.J. was explaining to the two thickoes crouched round him just what it did.

'It's a DFM,' he said and looked at their dim faces. 'It's an eavesdropping machine. You point it at a window and you can hear what they're saying inside. You can hear people moving about, even hear their clothes rustling.' Their eyes shone. Now they knew how they were going to catch the mysterious intruder.

P.J. elaborated. Speedy and Fraser would be on the inside with one walkie-talkie, Duncan and Jemma would be outside with another. P.J. would guide them from room to room, checking *in advance* where their quarry was moving to. When they finally got him cornered in a room they could lock, bingo! Fraser would call Geoff and they would all get medals. Speedy was doubtful but P.J. assured him it would work. Duncan had a brainwave – they could test it.

'Where?' asked P.J. and they all looked at each other and then at the nearest house they knew with people in it. Speedy and Duncan grinned wickedly.

'You must be joking!' P.J. groaned but they weren't, and ten minutes later, he found himself crouched in the bushes pointing his infernal machine at Debbie and Jemma's window.

Inside the girls were discussing this and that, as girls do, indeed as everybody does. They might not have talked quite so freely if they had known that every word was being listened to. P.J. slowly turned pink as Jemma and Debbie discussed someone he knew quite well. Himself! Jemma was asking Debbie if she fancied P.J. and telling her it was definitely not decent getting undressed in front of his photo – she ought to turn it to the wall. This last bit was also heard by Duncan and Speedy who nearly wet themselves laughing, especially when Jemma went on to give Debbie some flirting tips – how to bat her eyes, stuff like that. Debbie got very sarcastic at this point and asked her little sister if she stayed up late at night, thinking these things up. The answer had Speedy biting his arm so as not to laugh and give the game away.

'Sometimes I do,' declared little Jemma seriously. 'But I get my best ideas in the lavvy.'

Outside the lads were in a heap, laughing, punching each other and taking the mickey out of P.J. for letting his photograph watch little Debbie Dobson take her vest off. P.J. went very red but he wasn't as displeased as he made out. And the fact that it was someone with as fetching a smile as Debbie Dobson made it even more acceptable. Anyway, at least they knew the mike worked.

Nicola left the letter for Paul with Mr Skerrett. He seemed to be about to ask her something about it, weighing the letter in his hand as he studied her. But, to her relief, he just smiled and said he would ask Paul to ring her as soon as possible. Then she thought of another possibility. Maybe Tyrone hadn't had anything to do with the fire, either. After all Paul seemed to trust him and anyone Paul trusted must be all right. She hesitated. She didn't want to go to the magic shop but, in the end, she screwed up her courage and walked across there in the gathering gloom.

She was glad, though, when she got there, that she couldn't make anyone answer as she banged on the shop door. Although she didn't know it, Tyrone was inside. He even gave up the chance to frighten her with the red-eyed skull and the smoke from the dry ice, and just crouched down in the back of the shop until she had gone away. He cursed to himself quietly. It looked as if there was more to Miss Prim than a sweet smile and a lovely body. He hadn't thought she would come to see him on her own and, not for the first time that day, he wanted to talk to Paul in a hurry. But Paul had gone to London and, knowing Paul, would be back in his own sweet time. Tyrone badly needed Paul for an alibi.

Nicola just needed Paul's arms round her. Both she and Tyrone were disappointed. Then Nicola played her last card and rang Donna. As ever, in a real crisis, Donna came up trumps. And she only said 'I told you so' three times.

They sat together in the Metro Centre. Donna had conned enough money out of her dad to buy a large supply of drinks and rolls, so the waitress wouldn't keep coming to cough loudly and clean the table every five minutes. Nicola told her the whole story in the first few minutes and then spent the rest of the time thinking of even worse things that could happen. Paul could come back and walk straight into a police trap, for example.

Donna could see another possibility which she didn't actually want to bring up, Nicola being her best mate. But Nicola thought of it herself.

'What if he's done a bunk, though? Paul?' she said and put her hand to her mouth. Then she knew she didn't believe it. She was beginning to think that the man in the shop had done the dirty on the two of them, though. She remembered the creepy way he'd looked at her the first time she'd gone there.

'You'll have to get him to admit it,' Donna announced. 'That's all there is to it.'

Nicola knew very well that Tyrone would swear blue was black before telling the police he'd given Nicola a fire bomb to burn a garage down with. She just wished Paul was back – she missed him so much. Donna didn't think he was all that great and told Nicola so. Now if Nicola had seen this hunk of meat called Bill who'd come down to the Grove, then she'd be in business, no danger. Donna flicked her fingers and whistled.

'I could have ate him with no gravy, honest,' she vowed and Nicola had a great deal of trouble not giggling right out loud. Donna was subhuman, no question. Here was her best and only mate about to spend the rest of her life in Holloway and all Donna could talk about was hunks! Donna was almost offended.

'I was only trying to cheer you up a bit,' she protested. And, to give her credit, Nicola was feeling a lot better than when she'd first arrived. Jim Bell would let her stay the night, and Paul might be back the next day. Things were looking up. All she had to do was ring home and make sure it was one of the kids that answered it. It was bound to be Jemma, anyway. Jemma always answered the phone because it's the best way of getting to know all the gossip. Nicola had lost three lads she knew of through Jemma quizzing them about their prospects before calling her sister to the phone. God knows how many others had packed her in without telling her why.

Talking of lads and hunks and fancying people, back at the Grove Spuggie was standing with Joanne adoring Bill's back all the way down the drive. He was absolutely stocious, mega bright and turtle waxed to a fine finish, in Spuggie's opinion. So he couldn't play chess to save his life. That was OK. She didn't want to play chess all the time, just most of the time. There would be occasions when Bill's other talents would have to come into play. She watched him go and whispered a silent prayer. At least, she thought it was silent until Joanne turned and looked at her with raised eyebrows.

'What did you say?' said Joanne.

'Nothing!' said Spuggie. 'You tell anyone and I'll kill you. And you keep your eyes off him, too!' Joanne giggled, fit to break elastic. 'He's gorgeous,' breathed Spuggie. 'Just you remember, I saw him first. If I can just persuade him to wait a few months, I'll be fine.'

Joanne shook her head and said that Bill was years older than Spuggie, at which Spuggie flew off her trolley and haughtily informed Joanne that some men preferred younger women. Then she pulled up some grass and threw it at her mate and they turned miraculously into little scuffling girls again, rolling over and over and not caring where their skirts flew or how much leg they were showing.

Later that night, the ghostbusting show was called off. P.J. and Speedy and Duncan went up to the Grove right enough at half-past ten, ready to flick stones at the girls' window if it was on. But they got the fright of their lives when they saw a huge man going all round the edge of the Grove with a flaming torch.

'OK,' Fraser said. 'We'll have one more try. Later tonight. After that, if we find nothing I'll tell Geoff and it'll be Bob Grant.'

They nodded glumly. It would be goodbye party too, for Geoff would want to know what they'd been doing and would worm the whole thing out of somebody. They set a time to meet later and do what had been agreed.

As a matter of fact Geoff would have been grateful for some kind of diversion. At that moment he was receiving a deputation. Bill, Joanne and Spuggie were standing in his office and Spuggie was unveiling her idea. Bill kept his face as straight as he could, which wasn't very, as Geoff wheeled and turned and ducked for cover and Spuggie shot down every one of his excuses with unerring accuracy. She didn't want much, she told him. She only wanted the use of the hall for a whole Saturday, fifty tables, fifty chess sets, fifty chessboards

116

and fifty chess players from local schools. It wasn't as if she was asking for the moon, she carried on. All she needed was a bit of help and she thought she might have got it from somebody like Geoff who up till now she had assumed was a *friend*. She was sorry to have bothered him, she went on. She'd just have to try down the Council offices. Maybe they'd have some people who were more forward-thinking there. She started to march out in a huff but Geoff called her back.

'Sit down!' he ordered.

Spuggie opened her mouth to argue and Geoff raised a finger sharply. She subsided. 'But, Geoff!' she wailed and the finger went up again.

'You've been talking now – ' he said, looking at his watch. 'You've been talking for fifteen minutes and I haven't understood a word you've said. I'm now going to ask this guy here who looks as if he might have a grain of common sense buried under that mass of blond hair.' Bill smiled and Geoff nodded at him. 'Tell me what's going on, Bill!'

Spuggie opened her mouth again, only this time it was Bill's finger that went up. 'Spuggie's met a chess champion, a grand master who's in town for some kind of exhibition. She reckons she can give him a game but he doesn't play kids on his own. So she reckons that if she can con him into doing one of these mass sponsored things, playing fifty kids at a time, she can singe his whiskers.' Spuggie looked outraged.

'See?' said Geoff to Spuggie and Joanne. 'Short, sweet. American. Why can't you talk like that?'

Because she was from Newcastle upon Tyne was why retorted the unrepentant Spuggie. Anyway this chess match would be a major publicity coup for the Grove and Geoff was never averse to a bit of good publicity. It would also be a very good way to keep Bill in contact with the Grove and with his half-sister. Geoff had thoughts about that, too. It seemed to be working but Spuggie would have to be kept in touch or she

117

would be feeling very cheated at the end of the day if and when Joanne went away.

So Geoff appointed Bill as chess committee chairman and Spuggie and Joanne as the two committee members and away they went. Before they left the office, Geoff asked if he should ring up the chess champion and try him out with a few dates, to see if he could make it. Spuggie looked at him as if he was mad.

'I've already done all that,' she told a startled Geoff. 'We're having it on the nineteenth.'

'What if I'd said no?' asked Geoff, knowing the answer already.

'We'd have gone over your head,' said Spuggie. 'We'd have asked Mary O'Malley.' And she swept out, followed by her fellow committee members. The largest and least influential waved a little at Geoff as he disappeared through the door. Bill Paul was enjoying himself.

Charley had just managed to snatch the latest red rose off the doorstep and pitch it into the privet hedge before her mother came out. Her mother looked at her with bright suspicious eyes as she put the milk bottles out and closed the door. Charley retrieved the flower and looked at it, exasperated. It was a joke, she knew that. But who did she know who had enough money to play expensive jokes like this? On impulse the day before, she had asked in a flower shop and had reeled out, stunned, when they told her how much it would cost to send anybody a red rose at this time of year.

She was idly tapping the flower on the glass of the telephone box as she dialled Dexter Dutton (the second part of the don't-let-Robert-disappear campaign) when she suddenly made the connection. Dexter was sending the roses! Just the sort of trick he would have learned from

Rettega! It all fell into place. He had the money. He had the reason. He had the stupid romantic ideas. It was Dexter!

When he came on the telephone, with his voice already husked a tone lower than the norm to be real sexy, she nearly laughed right out loud. She didn't, though. She wanted a favour from Dexter and you don't get favours from lads you've laughed at. So she used her very best little-girl-please voice and batted her eyelids through the telephone until he was nearly trying to get in his end of the line and come down and see her. Then she asked him for the favour. It was like selling cakes to rich little boys.

'I've had second thoughts, Dexter,' she breathed at last. 'You've persuaded me. But I want to pick the song.'

Dexter took the bait. His voice went even deeper. 'Come along in, honeychile,' he whispered. 'Any time. Your time is my time.' He would probably have been there still, doing deep breathing exercises into the telephone, if she hadn't said yes and put the phone down at her end.

Fraser stood hesitating in Geoff's office and Geoff looked up puzzled from the list of repairs to be done. Fraser didn't usually seem unsure of himself. This time he was, because he was about to do something not quite sensible but far too exciting not to have a go at. His natural wariness made him want to take out some insurance against things going wrong.

'Will you be at home, tonight?' he asked. Geoff nodded and Fraser started to go.

'Is there something I should be taking an interest in?'

Fraser just asked Geoff to trust him and Geoff groaned inside. 'Trust me' is the first big lie in showbusiness, along with 'the cheque's in the post'.

The Famous Five gathered later on, having skipped out of

their houses at the pre-arranged times, Jemma in agonies about whether or not to wear a skirt so Duncan could see how thin her legs were getting. Nicola had rung to say that she was staying at Donna's and Debbie had told her mum, who had then told Debbie that if her sister rang again, she was to ask her to get in touch with PC Grant. It didn't sound important and so Debbie forgot all about it. She and Jemma mused about Paul and Nicola all the way up to the Grove but came to no conclusions except that there was probably no future for two vegetarians. They would die out for lack of meat after a couple of generations, according to Jemma. Look at dinosaurs.

All this was forgotten when they got to the Grove. Duncan, Speedy and Fraser slipped inside, using Fraser's keys, and prowled from room to room with the walkie-talkies, while P.J. tracked ahead of them with the DFM. There was nothing for about half an hour until P.J. stiffened and waved an arm at Debbie. In his earphones he heard definite running footsteps. He moved the mike along quickly and soon worked out the direction the feet were taking. He relayed swift and breathless instructions through Debbie and the walkie-talkie, while Fraser and the others hunted the feet relentlessly right up to the top of the building and into the very last room of all before the roof and the skylight. They burst in triumphantly, all fear of caution gone, but what they saw stopped them stone dead, their faces white.

Fraser told Duncan and Speedy to stay exactly where they were, and he flew down the stairs to the telephone. Geoff came out of his house at a scramble, shoeless and panicking, and drove way above the speed limit. Jemma and Debbie and P.J. waited, totally bewildered. A sudden movement made them turn and stand quickly. Behind them, holding a big shotgun, was the man from the gypsy camp and behind him, grim-faced, stood Mrs Finney, her eyes dark with worry.

Geoff surged out of his van, barged through the small group and up into the room where Speedy and Duncan still stood, silent and fascinated. Geoff went down on his knees by the little crouched figure that was scrunched into the corner. He turned to see Fraser framed in the doorway and behind him Mrs Finney and the big man.

'Ambulance, Fraser. Quick!' called Geoff but Tabitha Finney shook her head and stepped forward and cradled her little son, Paget, in her arms. She spoke over his shoulder to Geoff.

'No need for ambulances, mister,' she whispered. 'We can look after our own.'

The big man stepped past Geoff and the young people and took Paget in his arms, tenderly. He nodded at everybody and started to go out. Geoff held up his hand but Mrs Finney talked to him for quite some while and persuaded him that the boy would really be better off with his own folk. She promised to keep a closer watch on him and Geoff had to be content with that. He knew for a fact that the boy would be better off in his mother's caravan than in care in a special school.

At least, that's what he said to Fraser later when he was telling them all off. Then he sent them home, with a flea lodged firmly in each ear. They were all fairly philosophical about this. It had been one good adventure, that was for sure.

CHAPTER SEVEN

The Grove was buzzing with rumour, fact and fantasy mixed in roughly equal proportions, so that half the members were convinced that a spy had been caught and handed over to MI5 while the other half concluded that an exorcism had been conducted to rid the building of Gill's restless spirit. This particular group was having a field day, with talk of spirit guides and ectoplasm and revolving walls, until Fraser got hold of the ringleader, a walking pimple called Billy Hewitson, and threatened to burst him if he didn't pack it in.

Robert was immune to all these rumours, having effectively withdrawn from all social activities. He had taken to sitting on his bed brooding, and Lou found him there one afternoon with a package which had been slipped through the letterbox. It was Charley's last throw. She and Dexter had taped a torch song which she hoped might bring Robert back. If it didn't, then it was a very good way of saying goodbye. Robert slipped on his personal stereo and listened to Charley's version of 'For the Good Times' sung slow and straight and painful with all the hurt she was feeling buried in the words. If you've heard the record, you know what she was saying. If you don't, it's a love song saying goodbye and thank you. Robert listened to it and only heard the goodbye.

Meanwhile Tabitha Finney agonised over her little boy. She hugged him close and asked him again and again why he had run off. He just gave her a blank smile and snuggled closer. As he did so, she felt a crumple of cardboard under his jacket and, feeling inside, brought out Winston's photograph which Paget had taken from the wall at the Grove. She looked at him, puzzled, and wondered again what it was that went on behind those strange little eyes. He just smiled and she suddenly had the feeling that there was some purpose behind all that had happened.

The following day, Geoff held a serious post mortem to make sure he knew exactly what had been going on. He lined up the ringleaders, none of them penitent, all of them feeling that they were really due some praise rather than the constant earache they were getting from Geoff.

P.J. said it again, slowly and patiently. They were making sure the place was clear so that they could have a disco to raise funds to buy a memorial for Gill. This was a good thing, surely.

Then Speedy put both his feet in it, taking a worldly tone as he explained what they had really been up to. 'Acid house!' he said, like a missionary explaining something to the natives.

Unfortunately Geoff had heard of acid house parties where the police had been called in and found lads and lasses under the influence of strange and exotic substances biting the legs off tables and eating police Alsatians.

P.J. sighed loudly and wearily. 'Shut up, Speedy!' he said and explained to Geoff that acid house was really just the music. It had nothing to do with drugs, nothing to do with the police.

Geoff was sorry they hadn't just asked him instead of going behind his back but they said he would have said no. He said he wouldn't and so they did ask him and he did say no, at which point they all looked at each other and pulled faces.

'Not without proper safeguards, anyway,' he said and they all looked a little more hopeful. That sounded good, so long as it didn't mean Mary O'Malley as bouncer and Geoff playing the records. Geoff nodded them all out and talked to Fraser about it. Could Fraser guarantee there would be no trouble if Geoff did give permission for a dance? Fraser nodded. Nae bother.

'OK!' said Geoff. 'Let us know when.'

Fraser looked pained. He couldn't actually tell Geoff when. The whole idea of a secret disco was that the customers had to think they were doing something that was against the rules. But not to worry, Fraser would sort it and keep Geoff well in touch. Geoff had to be content with this and, anyway, he soon had something else to worry about.

The telephone rang and it was Bob Grant, the copper, on the other end, being very cagey but saying to Geoff that it was very, very important that he get hold of either Paul Skerrett or Nicola Dobson quickly. Neither of them was on the premises and nobody knew where they were, not even Jemma or Debbie, who knew very well but had decided they weren't going to shop their own sister, no matter what she'd done.

The day came and went. Nicola was still holed up in Jim Bell's pub, with Donna nipping out now and again to telephone for her to see if Paul was home. Each time that he wasn't, her gloom grew deeper, and Jim Bell began to wonder just what was up. He was going to ask her at one point but all hell broke loose in the pub and later on in the car park. A couple of coppers had come in and were standing round looking important. A crackle had come through on one of the personal radios and one of Jim's customers had seen the boys in blue, jumped up and sent half the clientele sprawling as he made for the door. The really stupid thing, as Jim found out later, was that the police hadn't been looking for this guy at all. They had been sent out to pick up a detective who was needed to go down to Plymouth and bring a prisoner back. But they couldn't ignore the flying felon who was so obviously anxious not to say hello to them. They pinned him down in the car park and found some very interesting stuff in his suitcase – some timing devices and some names and telephone numbers of garages and the tape recording of a demand for money with threats. 'Hello,' the message said. 'Send me some money now or I'll come and burn your garage down.' Or words to that effect.

All this would have been of interest to poor terrified little Nicola who jumped a mile every time anyone came into the pub. In the end, though, Donna got fed up being cooped up in the bedroom and persuaded Nicola to come down and have a last listen to the jukebox while her dad bottled the shelves up for the following day. Jim turned as they came in.

'Ring your mam, Nick, will you?' he asked. 'She's been on twice. I didn't know you were upstairs.'

Nicola pulled a face and Jim grinned. In his growing up days he'd been a bit of a tiger himself and there were times when the last thing he would have wanted to do was speak to his mum and dad.

'What's the matter?' he joked. 'Forgotten the number?'

Nicola just pulled another face and dialled home with a heavy heart. Jim started to tell Donna about the excitement earlier but she wasn't taking any notice until he mentioned arson. She grabbed his arm.

'What did you say?' she shouted. 'Nick! Listen!'

Jim looked from one to the other. He had no idea what was going on. But he told them obligingly that the police had arrested the man who had been burning down garages right in Jim's own car park. Nicola's mouth dropped open. 'Who was it?' she breathed. Jim didn't know his name. He knew who he was though. Dropped in every night regular as clockwork for a barley wine and a look at the Sporting Pink. Had some kind of joke shop over at Backleigh. Jim knew this because the fellow had brought a Dirty Fido in and slipped it into a woman's gin and tonic and got barred for a week once.

The grin on Nicola's face went twice round her head. You could have made toast on it for a family of four. She rang her mam at once and Jim shook his head. He didn't think Dirty Fido jokes were the slightest bit funny, although this one seemed to have cheered the girls up. Nicola felt exactly as if somebody had lifted a ten-ton weight off the back of her neck.

But later on, as she lay in bed wide awake, it didn't stop

her worrying about Paul who was a very good friend of Tyrone's, it seemed, and still mixed up in this affair somehow.

Joanne and Bill were growing closer and closer. Spuggie could see what was happening and she was getting more and more jealous. As they walked out of school, Joanne gave a little hop and a skip and Spuggie looked at her sourly. 'If Bill smiles at me tonight,' she ordered, 'you say you've got to go somewhere.' Joanne grinned. 'I'm not joking,' stated Spuggie angrily. 'He's never going to ask us out with you hanging round.'

Joanne just grinned again. Spuggie was in cloud cuckoo land. Bill would never ask either of them out. He was just the nicest person that Joanne had ever met and it was mega supreme with double anchovies that he could take the time out to bother with two snotty-nosed little schoolgirls. She saw him coming and raced to meet him, with Spuggie shouting at her in a low whispering growl. It didn't make any difference. Joanne grabbed hold of his hand and swung round him in sheer exhilaration.

Bill smiled and looked at Spuggie's grim frown. 'Hi, guys!' he said. 'What's happening?'

Bill knew how to clear the wrinkles from Spuggie's forehead. He just said he had a great surprise in store and they should change their socks and meet him later. Spuggie nodded to herself. She'd tie Joanne up and lock her in the airing cupboard and go off with Bill on her own. Maybe tonight would be the night he'd ask her out. She'd give him every chance anyway. She'd wear her shiny jacket. It was Joanne's actually, but if Joanne was tied up in the airing cupboard it'd be too hot for a shiny jacket. She skipped a bit with the thought.

Back at the Grove, Geoff looked at Bob Grant with dismay. He couldn't be serious, surely. Grant nodded. He needed to see Nicola. Very quickly. Geoff wanted to know what she'd done and Grant said it wasn't what she'd done so much as who she'd been with. Geoff knew at once who they were talking about. Beady-eyed Skerrett. Geoff wished he'd paid more attention to his first impressions but people always say that, with hindsight. Grant wouldn't say what Skerrett had done or even if he'd done anything at all. But he left Geoff feeling very edgy.

When Fraser came in straight from school, Geoff took him into his confidence. As always, Fraser was a mine of information. His school was full of rumours, as schools always are, and the latest gem was that the Green Brigade had been sticking placards on the windscreens of big cars. Fraser's lips tightened, a rare sign of emotion. One of the vandalised cars had belonged to the doctor who was patiently and carefully treating Fraser's mam in the rehab centre. If Paul Skerrett, or Nicola for that matter, had messed around with that particular car, Fraser was in line to tell them their fortunes.

'Just bring them here to me,' ordered Geoff. 'Either one or both, OK?' Fraser nodded.

Nicola had taken her courage in both hands again. Nothing if not persistent and utterly loyal, she was about the only person in Newcastle who had complete faith in Paul. She went to the vicarage a second time. As she marched up the path, Mr Skerrett happened to look through the window. He could almost hear the sound of a distant drum she was marching to and he groaned. He had wished more than once that Paul didn't attract such beautiful, painfully open and honest young girls. It was bad enough feeling the pain himself. It was much worse watching the effect his son had on the children that followed him and his cause. The vicar knew why Nicola had come, of course. She had been used and deserted, like one or two before her, and Mr Skerrett was determined this time that she should be disillusioned about his son as quickly as possible.

Tessa was in, about to go off for her Bible class. He asked her to probe gently. Tessa knew all about Paul. Mr Skerrett let Nicola in and went to make some tea. He hadn't been in the kitchen two minutes when he heard the door slam violently, rocking the whole house.

When he got back into the front room, Tessa bit her lip at him, her dark eyes sorrowful. She had started, as gently as she knew how, to tell Nicola that Paul wasn't all he seemed to be. Nicola had just stood for a second, stony-faced. Then she had told Tessa that all she wanted was to speak to Paul and would Tessa please ask him to get in touch. Then she had slammed out.

Skerrett was a little rueful. He should have handled it himself and he would, if he was given a second chance. He couldn't let Paul ruin any more young lives.

Nicola was still a bit wary about being seen in public and being asked the inevitable snide questions about where her boyfriend was keeping himself these days. So she stuck with Donna, who had run out of questions by now, and they haunted the far end of the Grove grounds.

Donna read the latest newspaper report on the fire which said that, far from being an ecological gesture it was 'believed to be one of a set of fires throughout the region.' And 'Listen to this,' she said. 'Blackmail involving thousands of pounds is said to be involved. So it's nothing to do with the Green Brigade. You've got nothing to worry about.'

Nicola pulled a face. Nothing except that she had put a parcel in a garage which had promptly burned down. And the man who had given her the parcel was now helping the police with their enquiries. Donna grunted and said she could carry on worrying if she wanted.

Then the ugly sisters arrived. 'If you've left home, can I have your bedroom?' Jemma asked sweetly, and Debbie chimed in with the news that the whole family was better off without her making sick noises whenever anybody ate any meat. Nicola and Donna walked away but it didn't stop Jemma and Debbie giggling. Nor did it stop Fraser collaring Nicola and telling her not to stick any more stickers on doctors' windscreens. Geoff arrived quickly to stop the row getting any worse. But before Geoff could ask Nicola about Paul and tell her to talk to Grant, she was off.

Jemma and Debbie watched with glee and a little fear. 'It's a major mistake getting mixed up with the fuzz,' announced Jemma. 'Once you've grassed someone up, they're all over you.'

Debbie looked at her. If her father ever found out that Jemma had been watching that very adult cops and robbers video, the fat would be in the fire. They were walking down the street on their way home now and were intrigued to bump into Bob Grant themselves. He asked them where Nicola was and, of course, they said they didn't know, not making the mistake of looking over Grant's shoulder where Nicola was quickly making her way off.

They watched him drive away. 'Soon as he claps eyes on her, he'll have her banged up in the nick,' Jemma quoted. Debbie shook her head. That video had definitely better go back soon. Jemma'd be getting tattooed next.

Something potentially exciting had happened to Duncan, Speedy and P.J. on the way back from the record shop. They spotted Paul with a rucksack on his back. He'd just got off the train from London and was telephoning Nicola. He put the phone down quite quickly when Mrs Dobson did something she didn't normally do. She asked him, very sweetly and persistently, where Nicola could get in touch with him. Paul

129

did *not* like the sound of that. Nor did he like the look of the garage he passed on the way to Tyrone's shop. He used some words under his breath which no self-respecting vicar's son should ever even have heard.

He didn't make the mistake of going close to the shop. He rang from the call box in the next street. No reply, even in opening hours. It was beginning to look as if Tyrone had been too greedy, once too often. He sat by the side of the road and thought about it. He had no illusions about Tyrone or the fact that he blackmailed garages for large sums of money. He'd been very generous to Paul and the Green Brigade. In fact Tyrone was the main reason that Paul didn't have to work. Paul didn't care why people stopped buying, selling and driving huge cars, just so long as they did. But now it seemed that Tyrone had done something stupid which might involve Paul a bit too closely. Also Paul didn't want to talk about where he had been that weekend. He had been on Brigade business which involved a brush with the law and he thought he might have been spotted, videoed, even.

He was also, to do him justice, worried about Nicola. She was much closer to him than his father and Tessa assumed. She was not like the others. Or maybe it was Paul who had changed. He certainly couldn't get her out of his mind and he had to get a message to her, quickly. He set off down to where he knew he could get his head down for the night, next to a small, hardly used business park, and he was aware almost at once that he was being followed.

Watching in shop windows and round corners, he soon realised who it was. He also had the chance now to get a message direct to Nicola. He let them go past, heads down like short-sighted beagles, and came up on them quietly when they were looking round in all directions wondering where he'd disappeared to.

'Lost him,' he heard the one with the stupid hat and the jive talk say.

130

'Not really!' said Paul and they spun round like round-abouts at Easter.

He persuaded them to give Nicola a message to meet him. They were quite cocky at first but a level glance from his cool grey determined eyes made them change their minds and they quickly went off to do his bidding, each one hoping that the others didn't think that they, for one, had been scared. They all knew, though, that they *had* been scared. Paul's fanaticism was very scary, seen close to. The boys didn't want to have to look at it again in the near future. Or in the far future, if it came to that.

Tabitha Finney was sitting in her caravan, watching Paget doing some colouring, and she was worrying about him. The life he led wasn't ideal. Gypsy kids needed to be self-reliant, cocky and muscular, able to deal with whatever life had to offer, and if it didn't offer anything, able to deal with that, too. The little children on the site were afraid of him. And the bigger ones were contemptuous, those that were big enough to know that there was something wrong with him. In truth, all that was wrong was that the boy was withdrawn – semi-autistic, if there is such a thing. A special school or even a remedial school would have spotted the problem. In fact any kind of regular school attendance would have made someone aware that Paget had special needs and that a lot of those needs could be fulfilled within the education system.

There was a little tap at the door and Mrs Finney was shocked to see the little kid with the glasses and the other one, the one with the dead friend and the candle. Then she got another shock; before anybody could say anything, Paget had bounced off the sofa and pulled Winston and Kelly into the van.

Winston looked at Tabitha. 'We just wondered how he

was getting on, like,' he ventured, and Tabitha was pleased as punch.

They sat and talked about lots of things and she could see her little weakling flower for the first time since she could remember. The other kids didn't pay him any special attention. If they had something to say to him, they said it, and if they didn't, they kept quiet. It didn't bother them that Paget wasn't bright. He was just part of the company. They all had dinner together – poacher's broth with hare and rabbit and all sorts of goodies, juniper-flavoured and steaming with garlic. When they had finished, they offered to take Paget down to the Grove and off they all went, hand in hand. Tabitha Finney didn't think it could be as simple as that but she had some hope in her heart for the little frail lad as she watched the three of them wind out through the dark, over-hanging trees.

P.J. and the other two passed the message on to Nicola as quickly as they could and told her where Paul would be. Bill took Spuggie and Joanne to a chess exhibition and, as soon as Spuggie was sure where she was going, she gave up all thoughts of making time with Bill and shot to the front to get as close as she could to the grand master and the game he was playing. Bill had taken the trouble earlier to make sure that the organisers wouldn't give her any trouble, but they were tickled pink at the thought of Spuggie.

Meanwhile Bill took Joanne off for a cup of tea and began to get to know his new sister. As they talked, she knew that she really enjoyed being with him, and part of her was already tampering with the daring idea that maybe she should stop being so scared and just get in touch with her father. Either he'd like her or he wouldn't. She looked at Bill – *he* was an American and there was certainly nothing wrong with him. She looked at him again and another superb idea butted itself through her brain and out of her mouth before she could stop it.

'Bill,' she started.

He looked at this dark little charmer and realised he would do anything for her. 'What?' he answered. 'Fair lily maid of Astolat, how can I help thee?' he added in his best English accent which made her burst out laughing and then look very cross.

'Don't take the mickey out of me, Bill Paul, or I'll have you,' she said, laughing, and he held up his hands for pax. Then he asked what he could do to help and her reply nearly turned him to stone. She asked if he would help find her father. He waited so long before answering, she was convinced she had offended him and tried to pretend she had just been joking. But he gave her his brightest Californian smile and told her that she had just employed the best father-finder in the business. She said apologetically that she couldn't pay much, and he had a hard time not letting her see how choked up he was. He recovered, though.

'You've got to promise not to be surprised whatever I come up with, OK?'

She promised and then started worrying. 'It's got to be my real father, you know,' she ordered. 'Not just some fellow who wants to foster someone. I've got foster parents already. What I need is to meet my real dad and it doesn't matter if he doesn't want me. I just want to see him, that's all. I can always stay living with Nick and Lou. They've already promised.'

He nodded, he promised. Then they went down to watch Spuggie hero-worshipping.

Nicola flew to the Arches to meet Paul. The message had been framed so that only she would know exactly where to come. He wasn't there, though, when she arrived and she walked slowly and despairingly through the tunnels and alcoves. Paul was there but didn't show himself until he was quite certain that Nicola hadn't been followed. Then he stepped out in front of her and she ran into his arms. Even while he stroked her back, his eyes were darting over her shoulder, checking, making sure. Then he held her away from him so that he could see her tear-stained, accusing face.

'Where have you been?' she sobbed. 'Why didn't you tell me?' She wept again and again as he tried to make her see that it had all gone out of control but it would be all right now that he was back again. She shook with sudden fear as she remembered something else but Paul was still talking and she had to stop thinking and listen.

'I swear to you,' Paul was saying, 'I had nothing to do with burning down the garage and nor did you.'

He sounded definite and she so wanted to believe him. It didn't make any kind of sense, though. She suddenly got angry and forgot all her tears and self-pity. She stared at him, right through his smile and deep into his eyes. She wanted to make sure she got right inside him, to make sure he was telling the truth.

'Don't treat me like a child,' she started. And her words stopped him in his tracks, stopped his easy, reassuring lies, the ones that always worked so well. 'I leave a package in a garage and it burns down! You disappear and I don't know what to do. Then the man that gave me the package gets arrested!'

He stared at her. Tyrone arrested? It couldn't be! He grabbed her arm so hard that it hurt but he didn't care and squeezed harder as she pulled away and squeaked. She told him again what had happened and he looked around quickly. There were a couple of people there, none of them taking any notice of the little scene being played out in front of them. The streets were becoming too dangerous for Paul.

He had to hide away but, more importantly, he had to leave town, and there were things he had to take with him.

He looked at Nicola, mouth half open, puzzled eyes beseeching him to make it all right. The anger had gone and she was a little girl again. No matter what Paul felt for her, though, he still had to persuade her to let herself be used.

'Think about it,' he said. 'Tyrone is in the mire, if he's been arrested. The first thing he'll do is tell the police I planted a bomb.'

He took her quickly and quietly to where he was going to spend the night and, coolly and without any compunction, set about winning her back again. It wasn't hard. She was in love. She just needed an excuse to believe him. They lay on his sleeping bag, warm and secure, his arms about her, and he told her that he had sometimes done things for Tyrone he wasn't proud of but you can't make an omelette without breaking eggs. He told her he had to go away and that, if she wanted, she could come with him. He would inherit some money on his eighteenth birthday. They could live on that till Nicola was sixteen and after that they could go and live with some friends of his on a secluded island in Scotland. First, though, Nicola had to take his key and get some things for him from his bedroom in the vicarage. She nodded and he put his arms round her and kissed all her fears away.

Spuggie got her autograph from the chess champion and bounced and laughed all the way home, while Bill grew quieter and quieter, the need to make a decision rising inside him like a flood. When they got home, only Robert was in and he was listening to Charley's goodbye on the tape, his eyes dark.

Joanne made coffee, Robert excused himself and Spuggie admired her autograph until, eventually, Joanne and Bill were alone for a while. He showed her photographs of the house in Foster City and pictures of himself and his other brother and sister, Josh and Charlotte. She looked longingly at the happy family and he took a deep, deep breath and told her. He gave her a letter, too, and she drew away, fearful.

'You asked me to find your father, Joanne,' he whispered. 'I've always known where he is. He's my father, too. Don't you want to read a letter from your father? Wouldn't you like to come and live with your real family ... and be Joanne Paul. Because that's who you really are.'

She looked at him and a great smile split her face and tears ran down both their cheeks as they clung to each other. Lou came in and saw them and fought back her own tears as hard as she could. Because she loved Joanne, too, and she knew she'd have to let her go.

On the other side of town the following afternoon, Nicola watched Mr Skerrett drive Tessa off to the Bible class and then she let herself into the vicarage. She went upstairs and into Paul's room and got all the things he needed. But then she found a photograph album and became engrossed in it and lost all sense of time, only becoming alarmed and turning quickly when she heard the knob turn and saw the bedroom door open slowly.

CHAPTER EIGHT

Mr Skerrett has been Paul's father for quite some time. In the past he used to give Paul the benefit of the doubt and, quite often, believed most of what he said. This was until he realised that his son was unscrupulous enough to lie about anything if it suited his purpose. Most of the time, the lies were intended to protect the aims of the various green organisations that Paul belonged to. But as the mainstream green parties were mostly peopled by gentle, caring, slightly woolly-minded souls who were opposed to violence in all its forms and couldn't appreciate the need for direct action, Paul soon fell out with them. And as he gradually moved towards the more fascist elements of the 'Save the Planet' lobby, so it grew more necessary to lie, and the actions the lies were to protect grew more anti-social and, all too often, more violent.

Whenever Paul went away without any warning, Mr Skerrett grew wary. Often Paul would come back quickly and unseen, take money or whatever else he needed from wherever he could find it, and disappear again, sometimes for months on end. He would turn up later when the dust had settled and his father would welcome him back like the Prodigal Son. Mr Skerrett loved Paul, even though he often despised the things he did and if he didn't welcome him back he was afraid he would drive him away for ever. It was the classic parents' dilemma. There are two solutions. In one, the sinner repents. In the other, the sinner doesn't. Regrettably, the parent sometimes has very little influence.

That doesn't mean the parent shouldn't do as much as possible to keep the damage to a minimum. Instead of driving Tessa direct to Bible class, Mr Skerret drove round the block and approached his house from the opposite direction.

He was saddened but not surprised to see Nicola going in through the front door, and he and Tessa went in after her.

When he opened the bedroom door, he smiled at her so she wouldn't be too frightened and was saddened again to see her face set in the mulish way that seemed to go with being a follower of his son. He asked her downstairs and settled her down with Tessa while he made some tea. Coming back into the room, he observed the way she sat, hands protectively round Paul's belongings, knees tucked together tight, head down, lips set, like somebody expecting to be interrogated. Paul had done his work well. The vicar watched Nicola again, weighing up what he knew of Paul, how much Nicola had been told and how much she should be told.

Tessa looked from one to the other. She knew and liked Nicola and didn't want to see her lose face. She also knew a lot more about Paul than anybody would have guessed and she still liked him; he was hard not to like. She didn't want to hear any more harsh words about him than she had to. She stood up and saw the quick surprise, almost anger, in Mr Skerrett's face.

'Can I go, please?' she asked and he shook his head. She sat down again slowly and against her will. He wanted support, she could see that, and he had been good to her since her dad had sent her to live away from the grim parish he looked after in South London, with its drugs and crime and low educational standards. (Her dad had been wrong, of course. The place was no worse than anywhere else but he saw only the bad and none of the good.)

Nicola was frightened. She wasn't sure that she hadn't been guilty of housebreaking or burglary or something, even though Paul had given her the key. She looked at the vicar and was startled to see his kind, understanding smile. Then she closed her mind quickly. Paul had warned her that if she ever met his father, he would confuse her and fill her mind with lies. He was jealous of Paul and his faith in the world.

The creed his father followed was empty and worthless and based on ritual and dressing up, Paul had said. All he had ever had for Paul and his friends was contempt and he would do anything at all to stop Paul following his chosen way of life, down to and including lying. Nicola was not to listen to anything he said. Nicola gazed stonily ahead. The vicar carried on looking at her understandingly but she couldn't keep quiet.

'Look!' she cried out. 'I know Paul's been stupid and got into scrapes and stuff. But all that's changed now.'

The man smiled sadly. 'You think so?' he asked.

'I know so! He's promised me!' She flared up.

Skerrett nodded and Tessa looked nervous. She had known other girls who had defended Paul with such conviction. She didn't know where they were now. She would be surprised if they were happy, though, wherever they were. Paul didn't leave much happiness behind him.

What Mr Skerrett was saying now surprised Nicola. 'Fair enough,' he said. 'I can't stop you doing whatever you want to do.' Nicola smiled in relief and stood up to leave but Mr Skerrett carried on and she felt her heart drop as she understood the truth of his words. 'If he's so honest and straightforward, though, why is it that you're here and he isn't?'

Nicola looked away but Mr Skerrett slowly and insistently made her face the one point that had never quite satisfied her even when Paul had held her tight and whispered in her ear. If he truly hadn't done anything wrong, and if there was really no danger except that of Tyrone telling lies about them, why had Paul sent Nicola to collect his things? She shook her head, confused, and he went on, choosing his words carefully and watching their effect on Nicola.

'Could it be, perhaps,' demanded Mr Skerrett, 'that he hasn't the courage to face me with whatever it is he's done now? To explain himself to me all over again.'

She looked at him, in the end, and told him what she

thought was the truth. 'Paul warned me,' said Nicola, 'that you'd tie me up in knots.'

Skerrett went to work again, this time including Tessa. He told Nicola that this would not be the first time Paul had been unable to face his father, that she was not the first girl he'd recruited to help him with his schemes, that there had been two others this very year, and Tessa nodded and Nicola wanted to press her hands over her ears and keep out this flood of lies and hate.

'I don't believe you!' she screamed. 'I believe Paul. He tells me the truth!'

Then Tessa cut the ground from under her with a quiet question, deep compassion for the other girl written all over her expressive face. 'Did he tell you about the island in Scotland?' asked Tessa sadly. And both she and Skerrett knew from Nicola's white face that this shot had gone home. 'Like he told all the others?' she pressed on, and Nicola turned away in anguish.

'It's got nothing to do with you!' she shouted. 'Nothing! So shut up!' They both looked at her and then at each other.

'There is no island, Nicola,' murmured Mr Skerrett. 'And whatever Paul told you about a future with him is lies, pure and simple.'

Nicola picked up Paul's belongings. Nothing they'd said so far could be proved. It just came down to a question of who she trusted, Paul or these two. And, on balance and because she loved him more than life itself, she would trust Paul until he did something that betrayed her trust in him. She told them both this and marched to the door. She would be safe with Paul and she was sorry that they couldn't believe that but she had her own mind to make up.

She had reached the door when Paul's father quietly asked her what she thought they could live on. Paul didn't have a job. She turned, eyes shining. They hadn't thought he would tell her or else they had forgotten about the money he was going to inherit. Her smile grew triumphant. 'He's coming into some money,' she announced. They looked at each other and Tessa shook her head.

'Ah!' said Mr Skerrett. 'You must mean the money due on his eighteenth birthday.'

Nicola was quite sure now that Paul had been telling the truth. She knew that his father would do anything to stop Paul getting the money his uncle had left him. And one way of stopping him was if Paul was in jail. Mr Skerrett was just jealous because his brother had left him nothing.

'That's what he's saying now, is he?' asked Mr Skerret and Nicola watched him open the case she was about to take away. He took out Paul's personal organiser and wallet and she started to protest when she saw what he was holding out to her. She looked at the driving licence, puzzled. 'He drives when it suits him,' said Mr Skerrett drily. 'But that's not the point. Did you know you could tell how old somebody is just by looking at their driving licence?' Nicola knew this, as a matter of fact. She had won a bet over her mother's age by producing her driving licence. The middle two numbers of the driving licence number show the year in which the owner was born. She looked at the date numbly, not wanting to believe what she was looking at. If the date was right, then it meant that Paul was ...

'Twenty-one two months ago. Yes,' said Mr Skerrett. 'A bit of a shock, isn't it? He's been trading on his youthful looks for quite some time now. Most young lads want to be taken for older than they are. But Paul is a lot cleverer than that. He does the unexpected.'

Nicola came out of the vicarage without the case, seething inside with conflicting fears and emotions. If Paul had lied about his age, it was entirely probable that he had lied about everything else. She couldn't bear to think about it, never mind talk it over, as Skerrett had wanted her to. But she

141

promised him she wouldn't do anything silly, and just walked away with her life in ruins.

Geoff suspected *his* life might end up in ruins if he gave in to Fraser. Fraser was proposing that they really did go ahead with a completely unsupervised disco. Geoff tried his fears out on Alison, who pooh-poohed them.

'The first thing they'll do,' he groaned, 'is head straight for the attic snogging and playing games.'

Alison shook her head. She knew better. She knew they'd be jumping up and down and playing the in band, Half Man Half Biscuit. Geoff looked blank and asked her to say the name again. It didn't make any more sense the second time. It was also a good job he and Alison couldn't see the two kids glued together at the mouth in the back of the coat cupboard right behind them. Or eavesdrop on a very interesting discussion, Jemma and Debbie Dobson were having.

Jemma lowered her head as Geoff went past. They were talking about the good time they would be having at the disco. It was already an established fact that they would be having one, but Jemma was drawing a few lines, beyond which she didn't intend to go.

'One thing I'm not doing,' she said, 'is playing Spin the Bottle.'

Debbie giggled. The Byker Grove kids played a very interesting and rather rude version of this well-loved game and Debbie knew exactly what had happened the last time Jemma had played. You spun the bottle in the normal way and whoever it pointed to, you had to kiss them. But if they were unbelievably dweebish, you could pay a forfeit instead. Jemma's bottle had pointed at Billy Hewitson. You couldn't get near his mouth for rotting pimples so she had gone for the forfeit. 'I nearly froze to death,' she squeaked and Debbie giggled again. It had been the highlight of Billy Hewitson's party, seeing Jemma go bright red.

Jemma changed the subject. Nicola had arrived, looking like a hen that's been out in the rain. 'She's going off the rails, you know,' Jemma pronounced and Debbie nodded. She was.

Alison had seen Nicola arrive. It's a pity Alison hadn't been taken into Geoff's confidence more but, because she was still mooning around, getting over Brad, he tended to confide only in Fraser for the time being. She went across to see if she could help Nicola, who understandably looked shattered.

'You want to talk about it,' asked Alison and Nicola looked round, startled. She didn't know it showed that badly. She sat down with Alison and, without going into details, told her that she had heard some things about her boyfriend. Alison's response was prompt. It was simple so far as she could see. Nicola should go to Paul and face him out. People should be able to talk about things, she told Nicola, a trifle bitterly, and then she gave her the clinching argument.

'If someone had been saying things about you to Paul,' said Alison, wouldn't you like your chance to put your side of it?'

Nicola nodded and quickly went off across the grass. If she'd gone down the drive things might have turned out differently. PC Grant drove up minutes later and went into the Grove. Alison followed him inside a couple of minutes later to see him patiently waiting and grinning while Geoff browbeat the establishment clerk at the Town Hall or some such place into lending him fifty tables, and then talked to the local newspaper about Spuggie's chess coup and asked them to send a photographer and a reporter. Grant turned and gave Alison a quick smile of welcome. He'd heard about Brad's defection and, like everybody else, assumed that he must have been suffering from a serious mental deficiency.

Anyone who passed Alison up for icebergs and penguins was headed for the funny farm, Grant thought to himself. She smiled back as Geoff finished his phone call.

'So?' said Geoff.

Grant looked awkward and proceeded to give them the worst piece of news to hit the Grove for quite some time. He told them that Tyrone had placed Paul firmly in the frame as his accomplice in burning Smythe's Garage down, and, worse, had said that Nicola was involved too. The senior officers handling the case had seen through a lot of his allegations and it sounded as if Nicola had been gullible more than anything else. They still wanted to see her, though, and it was more vital than ever that she be kept as far away from Paul as possible. Grant had been down to the vicarage and got the clear impression that the vicar had done his best to convince her that Paul was lying. This was a good sign, but Nicola wasn't at home and Grant wanted to talk to the kids to find out where she was and what she knew.

Alison looked more and more unhappy as this story was recounted. Geoff was shaking his head. Everybody knew that the cobbler's bairns were the worst-shod but it was hard to believe that a vicar's son could be mixed up in arson and extortion. Then Alison told them about the advice she had given Nicola. Geoff swore at her for the first time ever and immediately apologised. It was his fault for not keeping her informed, he knew that. The important thing now was not to shout at each other but to find out where Nicola was and get her away from Paul.

Nicola was at the Arches, looking distressed. She had shot straight to where Paul had promised he would be, but there was no sign of him at all. Until she looked more closely at the wall and saw a little message scratched in code which told her he would be in the business park next door.

Paul was sitting in an empty watchman's lodge, trying to come to terms with a strange feeling. Strange to Paul Skerrett, that is, but quite common to a lot of human beings. He was thinking of somebody else's welfare before his own. He realised that he desperately did not want anything to happen to Nicola and he cursed himself for sending her for his stuff. What if his father had caught her? What if his father had then told Nicola the truth about him? That was two-edged. If she knew about the sort of person he was, she would stay away from him and needn't get caught. If she didn't, if she came back, he would be faced with telling her himself.

Nicola walked slowly and nervously through the modern, sterile, mainly empty buildings that made up the business park. She jumped as a piece of stiff paper was caught by the breeze and rattled past her. She heard a hiss and turned sharply but there was nothing behind her. Down a little dark passage between two buildings, she thought she saw a flicker of light and started off towards it. Before she got there, a door opened quietly beside her, a hand slid across her mouth and she was pulled swiftly through.

Geoff had gathered the kids together and told them, without elaboration, that he would like to get hold of Nicola quickly. She would probably be with her boyfriend and did anyone have any idea where they might be? There was a sort of scuffling of shoes and a shuffling and a few pairs of eyes refused to meet Geoff's. Kids don't grass, it's as simple as that, Fraser murmured in Geoff's ear. So Geoff, Grant and Alison went back into the office and waited while Fraser got hold of P.J., Duncan and Speedy. He soon found out where Paul had last been seen.

Meanwhile, Grant and Geoff held a council of war. Grant said he had no alternative but to radio base. Paul had a record of fire-setting, according to Tyrone's confession. It was vital he didn't set fire to anything else. And if Nicola was found with him, she would have a lot of trouble persuading the police of her innocence. Geoff bargained with Grant. Let he and Geoff and Alison get right close to where they thought Nicola might be. Then let Grant radio in, giving Alison and Geoff a chance to get the girl clear. Grant thought this was very iffy but agreed in the end, much against his better judgement and hoping it wasn't going to backfire all over him.

Nicola sat opposite Paul looking directly into his eyes. They seemed to look the same whatever he said, she thought. Lies or the truth, he still looked painfully honest.

Her voice shook a little as she asked him the most important question of her young life. Was what his father told her true? He tried to laugh it off at first but then he looked at her face, made thin with sadness, and was serious.

'Probably,' he said. 'I don't know everything he told you but he doesn't tell a lot of lies.' He grinned bitterly to himself. 'Except he insists that there's a God, of course.'

She watched him and suddenly she could see the cracks in him. She saw things that hadn't been there before when she was so much in love. His expression was slightly cruel sometimes, his eyes flickered uneasily and his smile came much too quickly, like somebody producing a bunch of flowers from behind his back but when you looked more closely the flowers were plastic. She asked him how old he was and he told her the age from his driving licence. There was another long moment.

'Why did you lie to me?' she asked, and her voice was so small that he had to bend his head close to her mouth to hear and was both sad and surprised to feel her flinch away. He couldn't believe she didn't know that he would never harm her and then suddenly he knew he had harmed her far more already than if he'd hit her with an axe. So he set to and told her the whole truth about Tyrone and setting fires and blackmailing garages for money even though it was money for the Green Brigade.

'I don't care what you've done,' she said, eventually. 'I love you, Paul. And that's the truth. I love you.'

She did love him much more, now that she could see the flaws in him, now that she could see the real Paul who was no longer hiding behind a smile and a kiss and a lie. Now that he was someone who stood there and told the truth about himself.

The terrible reality of what she was saying made Paul rock slightly. He wasn't ready for the enormous responsibility of being loved for real. He took her by the shoulders, turned her round and opened the door.

'Go back and start the rest of your life again, Nick,' he whispered. 'You don't need me!'

She pressed hard against him. 'I do!' she said. 'I want to go to your island. I want to be with you. I want to live with you.'

'Just for now you do,' he told her. 'Because you think it's romantic and because I've told you the truth for once. I can't guarantee to tell the truth all the time.'

When she asked him why, he just shrugged. It was the way he was.

'And I'll never change,' he said, suddenly, angrily. 'Never!' He walked her out through the door, saying as they went, 'Come on. I'll take you back to the road.'

She hesitated a little but she could read the truth in his eyes and it was at that moment that she started to grow up. As luck would have it, this was also the moment that Grant drove round the corner high above and spotted the two small figures at once. He signalled Geoff to go right while he went left, and radioed frantically as he ran to get round behind Nicola and Paul who were standing together in a little world of their own. She smiled at him and brushed his cheek with her eyelashes. He remembered teaching her about that and what it was called, a butterfly kiss, and he thought just a little about what he was doing. He held out his arms, holding her away from him and trying to remember her face for ever. He kissed her and she began to cry and his resolve weakened again. But then he looked over her shoulder and saw the policeman coming. He thought she'd turned him in and his face twisted.

'Nice one, Nick,' he gritted and turned to run the other way, finding Geoff's hard pot-bellied bulk right up behind him. There was nowhere to run. He looked at Nicola cynically but she shook her head.

'I didn't!' she cried. 'I didn't tell them you were here!'

Geoff told Paul it was the truth but Paul was all about wiping the slate. He heard the police car wail and said bitterly that this ought to teach him not to hang about with silly little girls. The heavy-duty police car roared up and the back-up detectives took him in. His only request was to be in a different car from Nicola.

Geoff put his arm round her shoulders and tried to comfort her. 'He was just hitting out,' he consoled. 'Hitting out, that's all!'

She nodded. Paul *was* hitting out, she knew that. But it didn't make what he said any less true. Geoff took her back to the Grove and then Alison took her home. The police would have to talk to her, said the chief jack at the scene, but he didn't think there would be much of a problem.

Jemma and Debbie watched their drawn, grey-faced elder sister being helped into the house.

'I wonder if she's pregnant,' said Jemma.

Debbie pulled a face. It was bad enough in the morning without people throwing up all over the bathroom. And where would they hang their wet tights?

They were watching from their bedroom and decided not to go down for the family question and answer session that was about to take place. Mum and Dad would be asking questions and answering them themselves while Nicola waited till they were fed up and went to bed. It was something Jemma and Debbie had seen before and they had never learned anything useful. They went back to discussing something far more important. Spuggie had let slip that the big party was on! Jemma's eyes grew rounder and rounder with the excitement of it all until Debbie produced the show-stopper. Not only was the party on, but Debbie had happened to run into someone who was really keen on her little sister so, out of the goodness of her heart, Debbie had invited him.

'Who?' said Jemma excitedly. She'd have to pinch Debbie's sparkly tights and hide them till Saturday when the disco was going to be. But when she found out who the surprise heart-throb was, she felt like pinching Debbie black and blue. Her rat-faced sister had only invited the walking pus machine, Billy Hewitson.

'Yuck!' said Jemma, gagging. 'His spots are running into one another. His whole face is turning into one huge pimple!' She looked at Debbie. She had to get her own back for this. She could not believe that she had invited BILLY HEWITSON!!!!!!

Jemma had a sudden thought. 'If it was a choice between a really hellish forfeit and kissing Billy Hewitson, what would you do?'

There was no contest so far as Debbie was concerned. No forfeit in the world would make her get next to the crumbling features of Billy Hewitson. She looked a little warily at Jemma. 'Why?' she asked and Jemma leaned across and whispered something in her ear.

Debbie felt herself getting hotter and hotter on the spot. 'You're joking!' she breathed but Jemma shook her head. She was emphatically not joking. Debbie was on the spot. However, she said to herself, and then to Jemma, if it came right down to it, she might even do that. Jemma put her hand over her mouth. Saturday might turn out to be very interesting indeed. She was fed up with always being the one that had to do the interesting forfeit. They rolled over and over and discussed what they were going to wear and who else would be there and how Fraser would manage it without Geoff finding out.

Fraser was going to manage it very well indeed, as a matter of fact. The only people who wanted an illicit disco were the kids. But if anything did go wrong, they would be the first ones to be terrified out of their wits. Fraser's plan was mega simple. While everybody thought the dance was going on completely unpoliced, Geoff would be tucked away in an upstairs room with a portable television set and four bottles of Newcastle Brown Ale, paid for out of the dance kitty. That way, the kids could be as naughty as they wanted to (which is not actually very naughty) and Geoff would be on hand if anyone, for instance the Denton wallies, tried to gate-crash and set fire to the curtains. Geoff had looked at the plan from all angles and it was one of Fraser's best – seamless and watertight – and Geoff would also be able to watch *Match of the Day* without feeling guilty about depriving his wife of the big movie.

Joanne had, in the meantime, been given room to breathe by 'big brother Bill'. At first, she had said these words quietly to herself from time to time to see how she felt. It was really strange in the beginning but now she was getting used to it. Spuggie was enchanted, of course, this turn of events removing Joanne from the field of rivals and presenting her with a very acceptable prospective sister-in-law.

Before he left, Bill had produced a letter from his dad which he wanted Joanne to read while he was back in London making a few arrangements. Joanne just held it for a couple of days and then read it. It made her weep and it made her remember some things which she hoped she had forgotten for ever.

Mainly it was the simple story of two people who had fallen in love amid the blazing ruins of a country at war and had lost each other. She got to the last page of the letter and read how Danny Paul had raced through the streets as the enemy army had moved closer and closer, shouting his love's name out loud. When she was able to read on, it was to learn that he had been knocked down by a frantically driven jeep and hurled unconscious into one of the last helicopters to leave. Many years later he had found her mother's grave without knowing that before she died she had given birth to Joanne and without knowing that Joanne had survived.

She put the letter down, went to the telephone and rang Bill in London. When he came on the line, she simply said, 'Bill, I want to meet my father.'

Then she ran from the room and straight into Lou Gallagher's arms. They held each other and cried and laughed all at the same time.

In London, Bill rang his father and his message was just as simple. 'She wants to see you.'

So Danny and the whole family started packing their bags to meet their new sister and daughter. They fixed it to be in Newcastle upon Tyne when Byker Grove was at its best. Bill rang Geoff and suggested that it would be pretty interesting for his family to see something like the mass chess tournament. A smile wrinkled across Geoff's face as he reminded Bill that chess had really saved the situation. It was only chess that had stopped Spuggie playing gooseberry the whole time.

The trip was arranged for the Saturday of the tournament which also coincided with the underground disco. There was no special reason for this except that, as Geoff remarked, Saturday was shot anyway and the place would look like a tip; might as well get it over with in one foul swoop. (Geoff tends to mix his metaphors a bit!)

On the day itself, there was a major panic as the time grew nearer and the table-carrying and bumping into one another became almost Olympic standard. Geoff kept asking how it was going and Spuggie kept telling him it would go twice as fast if people didn't keep asking how it was going.

'Don't forget,' he told her. 'We have to give Joanne a major big send-off with her new family.'

She rolled her eyes. Of course she wasn't going to forget something like that. Geoff was a divvy sometimes.

Speedy and Duncan approached Fraser who was skilfully directing traffic. They were worried about the disco and more than a bit concerned that they would get their knuckles rapped if it went wrong. Fraser just gazed at them blandly.

'Not to worry. All under control,' soothed the thin lad with the glasses and the commanding air. They went away a bit happier.

Then Spuggie came steaming up to Fraser. 'Stop chatting with those layabouts, Fraser,' she screamed. 'He'll be here in ten minutes.'

He turned the same bland stare at her and asked her what else there was to do. She thought for a minute and then told him it was all done.

He grinned at her and smiled his most annoying smile so she put her tongue out and stumped off.

At home, Joanne was worried about the time too. She kept looking at her watch and then a sudden thought struck her.

'What if he doesn't like me?' she asked but Lou just patted her on the shoulder and said that if he didn't like her, he was too stupid to be her father anyway. Joanne grinned. She knew that if Bill was anything to go by, there wasn't anything to worry about.

Meanwhile, the Paul family hooted and cheered and sang the kind of songs families sing in cars as their big hire car with the steering wheel on the wrong side ate up the miles on the way to Newcastle. Being used to fifty-five miles an hour, Ellie Paul was terrified by the speed of the traffic but she didn't say anything, and the fields and cars and trees and little cows swept by in a comforting blur. Then across the big bridge and deep into the heart of the funny little streets; a knock at a doll's cottage door and they were all looking at a shy, frightened, desperately eager-to-please Joanne and, with just that one look, everybody's fears disappeared. Nobody said much. There was a lot of nodding and smiling and little quick looks and, at some time, they must have eaten but nobody could have said what it was except Lou, who made it and served it. They all piled into the car and went to look, first at Newcastle upon Tyne and then at the extraordinary place which was Byker Grove.

At the start of this story, everybody was worrying and planning a memorial to Gill. They should have realised that they didn't actually have to. All they had to do was look around them to see that there was already a better memorial in place than anything they could raise money to buy. No piece of stone or engraved metal or silver cup or pompous words on a certificate could do more for Gill's memory than the place itself which is suffused with love and friendship and all those things which, if you say anything about them to Geoff, cause him to go slightly pink and extremely gruff. Gill's memorial will always be Byker Grove. Even if the building falls down it will live on in the hearts and minds of countless solid citizens who went there as young people; Byker Grove, the place where children are given a chance to learn how to grow up.

The day of the chess tournament and the naughty things

that followed typified everything that was good about the place – high drama, low comedy, earnest searching after perfection, music, scandal, falling in and out of love, hellos and a memorable farewell.

The Pauls walked around the Grove, entranced. Joshua and Charlotte were starting to wish the whole family could relocate to Newcastle rather than just take Joanne to Foster City. Danny watched the heads of the dedicated chess players bent over the boards and looked at Geoff's proud grin as he made his way among them, not really knowing how they were doing against the grand master but knowing that he was proud of each and every one.

Joanne searched for the one head that meant more to her than any of the others and found it at one end of the long corridor at the top of the building. A stray ray of late summer afternoon sunshine caught the red curls and it looked as if Spuggie was aglow, haloed with light. She was locked in taut battle with the grand master who had seen off all the little challengers but now realised that he was meeting something more than a kid with a hobby. She was being pushed back, of course, but she was resisting with a fierce mature determination, skipping her knights from side to side, twisting and turning, never being forced into sacrifice but keeping the board as crowded as she possibly could, knowing that his superior endgames would always be her downfall but prolonging the moment as long as she possibly could.

She nodded absently when Joanne said she was going to America, and held her cheek up for a little peck. Joanne grinned to herself and pecked dutifully. She knew this wasn't goodbye, only see you. And she went down and the whole Grove gave them the send-off of a lifetime, roaring fit to bust. Spuggie did lift her head a little at that but the game had her totally engrossed and she got back on with it. When he finally had her beaten, the grand master offered the draw but she beetled her eyebrows at him.

'Don't you dare!' she said angrily and he nodded, angry with himself, and check-mated her. Then they both shook hands formally and he gave her his card, bowing slightly. She did the same, like opponents and samurai.

'Next time,' he said, 'it will be just you and me and not the circus.'

She nodded, fulfilled, and gave him her telephone number.

Then she went downstairs and realised that Joanne had gone and was sad for a while. But, like Joanne, she knew they would see each other again.

They all went home and the surrounding houses seethed with anticipation. Parents all over Newcastle looked suspiciously at their unbelievably obliging offspring whose unusually bland, co-operative behaviour rang alarm bells from Whitley Bay to the Tyne bridge. It would have been disastrous to be grounded on the night of nights so everybody perfected his or her version of Uriah Heep – rubbing hands, washing dishes, walking dogs and TURNING RECORD PLAYERS DOWN, and in general causing a lot more heartbreak than if they'd just racketed round as usual. Still, they all made it, just about, except for a minor crisis in the Dobson household.

Kath and her husband and Nicola had just endured a very bad time with a very senior police officer who had put the fear of God into the three of them before telling Nicola that the police would not be taking any formal action against her, after all.

As a result of this, Kath was behind with the washing and, for a horrible brief moment, it looked as if the girls were going to have to go to the disco in their school underwear. The day was saved, though, when Kath did a special load of whites only and let them use the tumble-dryer in the launderette which was much bigger and quicker than the little one at home. Her husband looked at her strangely and said that it was a lot of fuss about underwear, for goodness sake, but Kath just grinned at him. She had been a little girl herself and, though she trusted her kids, she also knew there were occasions other than getting run over when navy blue school knickers would be a major disadvantage.

And so the scene was set and the game was afoot. Knots and gaggles of brightly dressed teenagers filtered their way up to the Grove through the evening twilight, looking for all the world like an exotic tribe, the girls in glossy shell suits and gleaming silvery tights and all the lads wearing bright T-shirts, despite the nip in the air. (For a Geordie, ten below zero is still no excuse for a sweater.)

In the room at the top of the Grove, a worried Geoff was being secretly installed by Fraser.

'I want my head examining,' he spluttered. Fraser just shook his head, and assured him that he personally appreciated what Geoff was doing and he personally would make sure that nothing went wrong.

The first sign of anything going wrong, Geoff told him, and he would be down quicker than the first pint on a Friday night.

That was it, the end of the talking to. Geoff settled down with his beer and the sounds of merriment from down below cheered him up considerably. At one point, they were chanting the chorus of a song and he listened hard, puzzled. Then he shook his head. They couldn't possibly be singing what he thought they were.

Down on the dance floor, they were bopping to Half Man Half Biscuit, following Nigel Blackwell as he roared out the chorus. 'I HATE NERYS HUGHES!' they belted out, even though half of them had never even heard of Nerys Hughes.

The whole evening went like a dream. Except in one case it turned into a little personal nightmare but even in that case the personal notoriety it earned for Debbie Dobson eventually became a sort of social asset. Nobody ever thought she was prissy again, that was for absolute certain. Even Donna's mouth dropped open when she heard.

It started with Spin the Bottle. Everything was fine until the Walking Pimple spun and the bottle pointed at Debbie. With a mounting sense of horror, she saw Jemma lean across and whisper into Billy Hewitson's ear. His jaw dropped open and he looked at Debbie. For one beastly moment, she thought the agitation on his face would explode all his spots. She couldn't kiss him, she couldn't. Jemma grinned.

'Kiss or forfeit?' said Billy.

She heard her own voice croaking 'Forfeit!' and then she heard the whole room gasp as Billy recited the unbelievable forfeit her sister had dreamed up. She got to her feet. She was scarlet already. But she did it!

Upstairs, the hooting and whistling and cheering and the fact that the music had stopped brought Geoff to his feet and charging to the door. Before he got there, though, Fraser was in the room, calming him down.

'It's OK, Geoff, all in hand, we're packing in now,' he soothed, but there was an odd, twinkling grin on his face that made Geoff suspicious.

'What was all that row?' he asked. Fraser grinned again.

'You don't want to know, Geoff,' he said and Geoff had to be content with that.

Later that night, Jemma and Debbie lay side by side in the bedroom. Both sets of eyes were as round as they had ever been. Jemma turned to her sister.

'I can't believe you did that!' she breathed and Debbie shook her head and grinned quietly to herself in the dark. She couldn't believe it either but she didn't feel too bad about it. Quite daring, as a matter of fact. The next question shot her bolt upright in bed.

'What if somebody had had a camera?' asked Jemma slyly

and a cold shiver ran all over Debbie. She now realised just how lucky she had been!

So, that's what happened.

Nobody ever saw Paul again, although Nicola thought about his blue eyes for quite a long time.

Alison thought she caught a glimpse of Brad one afternoon at the end of the year but she wasn't sure and she didn't care either.

Robert and Charley finished, finally, and she never found out who sent the roses.

Winston came to grips with Gill's death and devoted his spare time to looking after Paget which made Kelly smile.

Carl joined the Army.

The nicest things happened to Fraser and Spuggie. Danny Paul had spent a lot of time talking to Lou about their troubles and asked her what would please them both. They could come to California in the future, of course, but he wanted to do something more immediate for them. So he paid for Lou and Nick and Speedy and Fraser and Spuggie to spend their first proper holiday about as far away from Newcastle as you could get and still be in England. Lou didn't want to go overseas with all its airport and passport and food and language problems, and the holiday was just as much a present for her as for the kids. They went to a little village on the Isle of Wight, called Seaview, and they stayed in a wonderful little hotel and Spuggie played with Pippa and Julia, the children of the hotel-owners and they let her ride their pony, Fable. And Speedy played in the rock pools and mooned over Charley.

The most surprising thing of all happened to Fraser. He fell in love with a girl who lived on a cliff. Her name was Emily Monk and he will remember her the rest of his life.

But that's another story.